HAN M GREENBARG

Snakebait Loves Shortbread

Contents

One

Heath

Wallet, keys, phone, spritz of cologne, final hair check. Oh yes. You're gonna take Parent Night by storm, Deitrich.

I grab my watch off the hallway table before heading to the door and glance at Diesel. He is lying upside down on the couch, entertaining himself with both the TV and whatever is on his tablet.

"Okay, dude," I say, "I'm taking off. Listen to Fern, and please, no bike rides in the dark."

"Can you get pizza on your way home?"

"I don't think it'll be open after the meeting ends."

"Then I'll take a milkshake from any place that is open. Thanks, Dad."

"You need to work on your negotiating, Diesel." I pick up his shoes from the floor and toss them into the basket by the TV. "Telling me what to do is not gonna get you anywhere."

"Remember how I said you should be more like Mom? Do it

with a late night food run."

"Just be good for Fern," I say. "I'll be back in a while."

"Yeah," Diesel mumbles.

"And one last word of caution, dude."

"What?"

I point at him and then at the kitchen, a dead serious expression on my face. "Don't touch my Creamsicles unless you want to lose two nights of game privileges."

Diesel rolls his eyes as he turns back to the TV. "Try harder, Dad."

Okay, so I'm lame at jokes. Dorky dad mode activated.

But I truly love how well-rounded and intellectual my kid is turning out to be. He has proven to be a genius in all things academic which means I almost never have to help with homework.

"Bye, Diesel." I wait for him to acknowledge with a head bob and then look at Fern who is sitting at the kitchen table with a thick paperback and cup of tea. "See ya, Fern. Thanks for watching him. Call if there's an emergency."

"Yup," Fern The Sitter says.

YUP, I think. That's the exact same response I gave to adults when they asked or told me anything that I deemed irrelevant. And today, at forty-one, I feel relieved to have passed through the turbulent wormhole of youth.

"And now," I say to myself in a goofy radio announcer voice, "it's time for a throwback."

I blast Linkin Park during the twenty minute drive to Diesel's school, singing a line or two when the urge strikes, blissfully accepting that I sound like a sick cow with the windows rolled down.

This is the type of situation when I miss having Lola sitting next to me. There was nothing quite like the fiery, flirty banter that only the most divine of women could provide.

But, lucky for my imagination, there is one other girl from my past that had the same electric energy. Cassie Wicker. I couldn't forget her if I tried.

Two

Cassie

"Thanks again for the treats, Cass. I know everyone will love them."

"Of course. I always appreciate an order." I start putting trays on the table and notice Ariana circling me with pursed lips and squinty eyes. "What?" I ask. "Did I forget something?"

"Just wondering if you brought the stickers for my class. I know it takes awhile for you to design them but that was three weeks ago."

"Right here." I pull out a small box from my purse and hand it to her. "Made sure to spell all their names right. Aren't the animals cute?"

"They are." Ariana sifts through the individually wrapped stickers before putting the box on her desk. "I'll pass them out on Monday."

I laugh at the speed in which she rushes past me to greet the arriving parents. Her perpetual teacher-type A energy somehow seems more apparent when surrounded by our fellow middle-aged adults. Rather amusing to someone like me who prefers my own company to being part of any cliquey group.

I'm a now and forever dorky introvert.

My attention goes back to arranging the desserts and drinks. I listen to the pleasantries being exchanged between the parents and Ariana, quite glad I'm not the one who has to sit through a two hour "turn to page twenty-five of this year's schedule" meeting. I'm hungry though. Part of me wants to try another of my cookie dough brownies just to be sure they taste as great as when I took them out of the oven an hour ago.

As I mindlessly stack and re-stack cups, pondering whether to eat a brownie or not, someone dramatically clears their throat behind me, and then I hear, "Well, well, well, if it isn't Sassy McVocab Queen."

I freeze as fast as a Coke in Antarctica, refusing to look over my shoulder.

That's his voice. HIS voice. Maybe he'll just walk away. Maybe he'll...

But he comes around to the other side of the table and meets my eyes. Instant flashbacks. Instant stomach drop.

Don't move. Statue. Just don't respond.

He leans in with a sly smile. "Hi, Shortbread."

HEATH. Heath Alun Deitrich. In the same room.

Few things in life faze me anymore, but encountering this guy twenty-three years after our last face-off is unprecedented. It should not be happening.

"Snakebait," I growl through gritted teeth.

"Oh!" he says in a teasing, upbeat voice. "You do remember me."

"Yeah." I look toward Ariana, wondering if she secretly set

this encounter up. But I wouldn't think she would be that cruel… unless it's just the bridezilla mode kicking in for her.

"Aren't the odds insane?" Heath says as he pours himself some iced coffee. "I have to say, Shortbread, you've hardly changed. Except the glasses. You didn't wear them back then, did you? And your hair isn't red. Guess you stopped dyeing it."

"Yeah, I stopped. And I really hope you don't eat all of those."

He tilts his head as he takes a brownie. "Why would I do that?"

"Eleventh grade. Chemistry. Mr. Randolt brought in a box of doughnuts for us to eat before the test and somehow you snagged and ate all of them."

Heath smiles and eats the brownie in one bite. He holds eye contact with me while sliding the cups around on the table, knowing how annoyed I'll get.

I'm not flipping out. I'm not that girl anymore.

I step away and fold my arms, leaning against the table's edge. "Still up to your old tricks, aren't you, Heath?"

"I try to be a good example for my son. But at times, yes, I may be quite juvenile." He follows me, placing himself just inches from my face. "And you, Cassie? Married? Kids?"

"Nope," I say proudly. "I'm free."

Heath smirks. "Are you now?"

"That's right. And I assume your woman is a longtime girlfriend since you aren't wearing a wedding ring."

"I could be married and not wear a ring. That's normal these days."

"Then you're married?"

The playfulness in his eyes turns sober. "No. We never did that. And she's gone. Lung cancer."

"Oh… I'm sorry."

He nods, pouring more iced coffee. "Yeah. But seriously, I love my kid. He's great."

"What's his name?"

"Diesel."

"Diesel? Who picked that?"

"I did. Took lots of begging and a sign from God."

"I bet," I say. "Men definitely know how to crank up the charm."

Heath shrugs and picks up a caramel fudge square. "Man, these are really the best refreshments I've ever had at a Parent Night."

I almost smile but hold myself back. "I don't think you realize it, Heath," I say, "but I made all these desserts."

His blue eyes widen and he flashes a half-smile. "Really?"

Shoot. The jerk's eyes are cute.

"Yeah." I look at his outfit— a teal button-up shirt and the cleanest jeans I've seen any man wear. His suave yet chill hairstyle. His cologne. He's aged better than I thought he would. "It's sort of my business now," I say. "One of them."

"You're a caterer?"

"Desserts, yeah. Just me and my own company."

"That's really cool, Cassie."

"Thanks."

Heath stares at me with his half-smile, piling three brownies into a napkin. He doesn't say anything else until Ariana calls for all the parents to sit down. "It's really nice seeing you." He nudges his elbow into my chest before sitting at a back row desk. "Shortbread," he whispers, slowly and painfully drawing out both syllables.

"Stop it. You know what that reminds me of, Heath."

He looks at me with a mocking pouty face. "But it's who you

are to me. It's funny and cute."

"No!" I explode. "That day was horrible! How can you make that mistake? How can anybody make that mistake? A craggy piece of shortbread stuck in my throat and you run over and plant a long kiss on my mouth!"

Heath intently listens. So does everyone else in the room. As embarrassed as I am about bringing the cafeteria incident up, I'm more angry at the fact that it's still so vivid in my mind.

"Heimlich, Heath! You were supposed to do the Heimlich! Ian had to jump in and save me instead of you."

"Maybe you shouldn't have taken that dare from Emily, you nutjob," Heath says with a laugh. "Scarfing down fifteen shortbread cookies in thirty seconds. I mean, that was dumb, and she was just trying to make you look stupid."

"The entire cafeteria was watching me. I had to see it through."

"And look how that went. You almost died."

"You kissed me while I had food in my mouth! With your tongue and everything! That is so disgusting."

"Okay, so I'm disgusting." Heath stands up and points at me with a brownie. "But you got me sent to juvie, Shortbread. Remember?"

My cheeks redden as I absorb the accusation. Heath and I have completely taken the attention away from Ariana's professional presentation, but I can't stop myself from ranting.

This has to be said.

"You were only in a facility for two weeks! It was supposed to scare you straight."

"And what did I do when I got out?" Heath asks calmly.

"You lit illegal fireworks on the school roof."

"I did. And I just got a normal day of detention."

"Plus ten hours of helping the janitor clean hallways."

"Yeah. Thanks. You know I despised the idea of community service."

"Well, it made you think, didn't it?"

"Yeah." Heath sits back down, eyes fixed on me. "I thought about how you kept ratting me out. Just once I had hoped you wouldn't be such a prissy whistleblower."

"You got off easy, Snakebait. Every time."

"Not when I got home," he says in a softer voice. "You never saw the other consequences."

Consequences. Really.

I may not have known everything about Heath back then, but he didn't know the real me either. His current body language is making him look like a poor, shrunken underdog, and he's getting sympathy stares from some of the other men in the room.

Fantastic. Why did I let my former adversary get the best of me again?

I shake my head at my irrational, out-of-character outburst, and quickly walk toward the door.

"Cass," Ariana says dryly, "thanks for the entertainment."

I don't bother to turn around, but I nod, shifting my purse to my other shoulder. "No problem."

"And don't forget about Wednesday. I'm finalizing the bridesmaid dresses."

"Got it." I exit the scene of degradation, sighing loudly as I move through the hall.

Just get home. Go to bed. It'll all be better tomorrow.

"Cassie, wait!"

Oh my fudgesicle. I drop my head and stop walking.

"Did I hear that right?" Heath asks as he catches up to me.

"What?"

"Are you in Ariana's wedding?"

"Um, yeah."

"Well…" He grins slyly. "So am I. One of Ian's groomsmen. Maybe I'll do a repeat of the prank I did at tenth grade prom."

My jaw drops.

He has to be lying. Joking, lying, teasing. Anything but that being the truth. Please, please, be kidding.

"Guess we'll be running into each other again, Shortbread."

Plain speechless.

I'm going to experience the most humiliating incident in the midst of my midlife crisis. At my best friend's wedding. The cameras and smartphones will be rolling during the ceremony and reception, and I can just imagine the back-to-back pranks Heath will pull on me. There will be no dignity left. And the videos of it will be posted everywhere.

"See you later," Heath says. He pokes me hard in the ribs like he used to do with a pencil in math class. "You look good in yellow."

As I watch him go back into the classroom, I'm overwhelmed by the same feeling I had every morning when I got to school. Pure dread. Always worried that I would be mercilessly picked on by Heath Alun Deitrich.

Turn the tables. That's all I can think of. *Prepare for the inevitable, retaliate, and maybe… just maybe… he won't get me this time.*

* * *

I change into a comfy outfit when I get home and have a cuddle with my collie Odessa. My late night routine usually consists of a giant bowl of Fruity Pebbles, and two hours of *Seinfeld* or *Everybody Loves Raymond*—thanks to my gaggle of retro DVD box sets. But Heath overrides every thought I have. Just like the old days.

"HEATH!" I yell madly at the ceiling, "your day of reckoning will come!"

For the greater good of all living things, the man must be dealt the hand of vengeance. Or I will turn into a bridesmaid from the dark pit of raging fire.

Three

Heath

It takes everything in me to focus on what Ariana is saying. I get the gist of how a school year works… pretty much the same as it was when I was a kid.

Well, except we didn't have the fancy tech that exists now. That would've been great for speeding up homework.

"If you have any questions you can send an email. Thank you for coming."

Ah. There it is. The closing statement.

I look around the room to see who else is eager to spring from their seats and realize I'm the only one who's halfway to bolting.

"Heath," Ariana says as I stride past her, "I'm certain your son will do well in class this year. But it'd be nice if you actually had paid attention to the rundown instead of fantasizing about Cassie."

"What can I say? I can't believe I got to see her after all this time."

"All you need is longer hair, a leather jacket, throw the piratey earrings back in, and you'd be the same guy who zoned out in all our classes."

I smile. "I'll take that as a compliment. Means I still got some youth left in me."

"All men have crazy youth in their eyes."

"Crazy or not, I have a question for you, Arry."

"Yeah?" She waves at a group of parents who are making their way to the door. "Is it about cutting out book reports? Because you know that's my favorite assignment to give."

"No. I want Cassie's number."

Ariana whips her head around, looking at me like I just uttered some kind of goblin language. "You ARE crazy."

"I'd like to reintroduce myself."

"You can do that at my wedding, Heath. There will be time to annoy her then."

"I'm not waiting all those months to be next to her again. Please, Arry. You and Ian know I'm a different guy." I almost get down on my knees to beg for the number, but I see a small smile on Ariana's lips and know I don't need to fight that hard. "Please."

Ariana shakes her head as she takes a scrap of paper from a drawer. She finds a pen and jots Cassie's number down. "You're the oil to her water, Heath. If by some chance you two end up getting along, it'll be against all logic."

"Zero confidence in my methods?"

"Maybe like seven percent. I'd like to see a happy outcome for you, but just don't be the reason that my wedding goes up in flames."

My excitement explodes when I take the paper. "You won't

regret this."

"I'm sure." She goes to her desk and sifts through a pile of folders. "Take care, Heath."

Wanting to bust out wacky dance moves but trying to stay calm, I slowly walk to the door. "Arry, do you happen to remember if Cassie said anything nice about me at all during high school?"

"Yeah. She once told me she thought you were the cutest guy on campus."

Woo hoo, I think. *You're the man, Deitrich.*

"I can work with that." I stare at the number in my hand, eager to plan our first phone conversation. "Absolutely can work with that."

Ariana follows me into the hall. "How do you know Cassie won't just hang up and block your number when she hears your voice?"

"Oh, I've got a foolproof way to keep that from happening."

"Yeah? And it's worked before with other women?"

I answer her as I walk backward. "Eighty percent success rate."

"What is it?"

"I ask a specific question."

"About?"

I turn around with a grin and silently make the journey to the parking lot.

"Heath? C'mon, tell me the question! It'll drive me nuts all night!"

I chuckle at Ariana's frustration of being ignored, knowing full well that she will ask Ian about it when she gets home. Ian knows my tricks. He'll tell her anything she wants to know.

"You got this, Deitrich," I say to my reflection while pulling onto the road. I turn on some Green Day and mouth the words to "When I Come Around", imagining how epic it would be to dance in the car with Cassie.

Cassie. My Shortbread.

I know she had a bitter sting in her voice when she called me 'Snakebait', but it couldn't have thrilled me more to hear that nickname again.

* * *

It's close to midnight when I get home. I send Fern out with her money, kick my shoes off, and check to see if Diesel is asleep. The kid is passed out with his tablet under his arm and his earbuds in… not the healthiest way to sleep but I'm just happy he is in his bed and not on the couch, and that he's not awake to ask me why I didn't stop at a drive-thru to indulge him with a midnight beverage.

The yearbooks, I think. *Gotta look at the teen Cassie and see if my memory was right about what had changed.*

I go to the lone bookshelf in the living room and seek out my yearbook from ninth grade. I flip through the pages, sliding to the floor, and pause when I see Cassie's picture.

Yup. I was right. She didn't have glasses back then. She had long, bright red hair. Little spitfire.

I smile as the memories swarm in, thinking how about how much we put each other through—the trouble went both ways. It was never all on me.

"Where's my milkshake?"

Diesel.

He always rouses from sleep at the worst times to pelt me with questions.

"Go to bed," I say.

"What'd Miss Layton say about me?"

"School has hardly started, Dees. What would she have to discuss about you?"

"Yeah, I know she already knows I'm smart."

I glance up at him. "Did you remember to brush your teeth?"

"I'm a fourth grader, Dad. You don't need to remind me anymore."

"I have trust issues with you. You fought me and your mom long and hard over the brushing teeth battle."

"I did brush them," he says, sitting next to me. "But you didn't bring me a milkshake."

"Of course not. It's midnight."

"It's the weekend."

"Still midnight," I say.

Diesel looks at the page I'm turned to and taps Cassie's picture. "Is that the girl who always got you in trouble?"

"Yes. But that was only when I wasn't getting myself in trouble."

We trade mischievous grins and continue looking through the yearbook. Just when I think we're gonna close it up and I'll get him back to bed, he says, "You should ask her out, Dad."

"What?"

"Yeah. You're always looking at her pictures on the computer."

Wow. My kid has no idea of how much I want to do that very thing.

Ask Cassie out. Yes, please.

"Do you have to make me sound like a stalker, Diesel? Those are public photos that I look at. Anyone can see them on her blog."

"Blog," Diesel snorts as he stands back up. "No one has blogs anymore."

"It is a blog. She's written monthly posts alongside her gallery of photos. It's all about her adrenaline-fueled adventures."

"Okay, Dad. Keep looking at Cassie's blog. But you should do more about it."

"Well, I did just get her number and I do plan on calling her."

"Can you call her now?"

"I'll call tomorrow, but convincing her to go on a date with me will be almost impossible. She's still worked up about things I did in high school."

"Show her you changed." Diesel pulls out one of my old comic books from the bookshelf and paces as he reads it. "I can help."

"No thanks, Dees. I'll figure out my own plan of action." I get up to put the yearbook back in its place. "C'mon. Back to bed."

"What does she look like now?"

"Geeky. Still very cute. She made desserts for Parent Night. Has her own catering company."

Diesel tosses the comic book in the air as we head to his room. "Can we order some cupcakes from her?"

"No."

"Why not?"

"Dees, I highly doubt that she would make time to bake something just for me."

"Does she have kids?"

"No kids and no husband. I wouldn't be trying to get to know her if she had a husband."

Diesel flops onto his pillow, carelessly pushing his tablet to the floor. "I don't think Mom would mind if you became best friends with Cassie."

"Really?" I chuckle, watching him pull the covers over his

head. "What makes you say that?"

"Because Mom's watching us every day from Heaven. She knows you need someone else to talk to and laugh with."

"What about tickle fights? You think I could get Cassie to get on board with those?"

"If she's at all like Mom was, then yeah, she might like the tickle fights." He pops up from under the covers and points a finger gun at the ceiling. "And make sure Cassie likes *Iron Man*. That's the most important movie."

"*Iron Man*? What about *The Dark Knight*? I thought that one was at the top of the list."

"Batman is your favorite superhero, Dad. Iron Man is mine."

"Right. I forgot."

"Will you ask Cassie who her favorite superhero is?"

"Sure, Diesel. If we ever get around to that subject I'll ask her."

I pick up a pile of dirty clothes from his closet floor, noticing that he's got more mismatched socks than I do. "Still going to Ryan's house tomorrow? I gotta work for a few hours so it'd be nice if his mom lets you hang with them."

"Yeah. We're gonna skateboard and game."

"All right." I turn the light off and the fan a notch higher. "Night, my dude."

Diesel's response is to bury himself under the covers, and I take that to mean he is checked out for the night. He likes sleeping in a chilly room to pretend he's on a trek to Mt. Everest. One of his new and ever-changing phases. *Funny kid.*

I back out of the room, closing the door behind me, and head to my makeshift laundry corner on the far side of the kitchen. Cleaning anything puts me in a happy zen mode. Women usually love it when they discover that aspect about me—a man who enjoys dusting, polishing, washing surfaces until they sparkle. I hope Cassie will be enchanted by it too.

Four

Cassie

My alarm sends me flying off the couch. Linkin Park's "New Divide". Forgot how loud I had set it and now I'm struggling to find my glasses. Odessa is giving me the side-eye from her plush bed, looking at me like I'm the most confusing creature in the world. Truly, I do feel confused. I had a dream about Heath last night and in that dream I kissed him and ran away.

So irrational and nutty.

"You're reading my funky energy, huh?" I say to Odessa.

Odessa yawns, stretches, and trots toward the doggy door that leads to the backyard. I observe her morning routine—first pee of the day, a perimeter check around the fence, and sticking her nose into several gopher holes.

Oh, the grand, simple life of a dog.

"Granola and yogurt. Granola and yogurt. Shoot! Where's the vanilla one?" I pull containers from the fridge, flinging them onto the counter, unable to find the vanilla yogurt that

I was so sure I had saved for this weekend. I think Heath has wrecked my whole sense of identity here. I don't even know what shelf I'm looking at right now.

Did I buy grape juice? I hate it. Why is it in here?

I talk to myself way more than I'm proud of and try to justify it by saying that I'm actually talking to Odessa as if she was a human and not an adorable fluffbutt. I mean, as a dog mom, I think it just comes with the territory. I turn on an episode of *Cheers,* sit with my bowl of granola and strawberry yogurt, and wait for the coffee to brew.

Just me and Odessa in this spacious house—sometimes lonely but it's always peaceful. The TV is typically on to keep both of us company. Odessa loves it as background noise too.

I'm in the middle of filling my mug with strong black coffee when my phone rings. The number is not one I'm familiar with, but it is in my area code and it's not a one eight hundred number so I keep to my standard answering procedure and swipe to accept the call. "Hello?"

"Hey, Cassie."

I cough up a granola cluster.

No, no, no. Oh no.

"Heath?"

"Yeah. It's Heath. Sounds like you're about to have a repeat of the cafeteria incident."

I groan when I hear him laugh.

Hang up on him. Just hang up.

"Listen, Cass, I would really like us to talk. Just you and me. We'll go out and catch up."

Hang up. Hang up.

I sip my coffee and almost slam the mug down. *Chipped the bottom. Shoot.*

Part of me doesn't want to hang up. Part of me wants to hang onto him. I'm not making sense to myself. "Heath, are you being serious?"

"Totally am."

I charge into the living room and check the windows to see if he's outside. "Ariana gave you my number, didn't she?"

"Well—"

"Why'd she do that?"

"Cassie, all I want to do is talk."

"No."

"Can I take you on a date? Please?"

A date?! He wants to take me out like I'm his girlfriend?

"No, Heath! Are you crazy?"

"No, I'm just—"

"Do you not feel my aggravation at all?"

"Just a little dinner date to talk. I'm not gonna mess with you."

It's a trap.

The fear of an incoming prank has me running up and down the stairs like a flustered chicken. "I gotta go. Don't call me aga—"

"Cassie, wait! Wait!" His voice is suddenly frantic. "One question and I'll stop bugging you."

I stop my sprinting back and forth and look at my snarling reflection in the downstairs bathroom mirror. "What is it?"

"Do you like dogs?"

Do I... I take the phone from my ear and set it on the counter. *He asks me about dogs? Where did that come from?*

I don't want to indulge Heath. But he brought up dogs. Dogs are the best thing we've got in this life.

"Cass? You still there?"

"Yes." I leave the phone on speaker and clear my throat. "I'm here."

"So, can I assume you like dogs?" Heath asks in a weirdly timid tone.

"I don't like dogs," I say. "I LOVE them."

"Yeah?" There's a smile in his voice. "You have a dog?"

"Her name's Odessa. She's five years. Collie."

"Odessa is a unique name. How'd you pick it?"

Heath is talking to me like he has all the time in the world. Like we're besties.

"Greek mythology."

"Clever," he says. "Wanna know the origin of my kid's name?"

"No."

"But it's a really funny story."

Hang up. You gotta just hang up.

I pour myself more coffee and take a big gulp before saying, "Bye, Heath."

"Cassie, can I—"

I tap end. Throw the phone on the couch.

Call over. Done.

I sigh and look at the time. Need to make a grocery run this morning before completing my two scheduled brownie deliveries.

* * *

The cereal aisle is one of my happy places. Strolling up and down it, humming like it's a lovely vacation destination. More than once I've been asked if I'm lost or if I need a mental health evaluation, but generally the staff leaves me to my pacing. You can't blame a girl for wanting to dive into every colorful box

23

and indulge in the admittedly unhealthy but addicting contents.

I toss a box of Trix into my cart and take my phone out to call Ariana—she's probably the one who gave Heath my number and is waiting around to hear about what he said to me in our short-lived phone conversation.

"Arry," I say, "Heath asked me out."

"Yep, I figured that would happen."

"You realize I'm not up for indulging my enemy, right?"

"You've been looking for another adventure, Cassie. You've said so a million times in the last three months. Let Heath be that next adventure."

"Can you promise he won't pull an idiot prank on me?"

"You have to let him prove that he's a good guy. Just pretend you're about to do a skydive and you'll get a burst of happy adrenaline."

Ariana is right about that. I will be feeling adrenaline. Just not the smiley exuberant kind. "I hate going on dates," I say. "My last date was a month ago and he wouldn't stop talking about his pill and hand sanitizer containers. He was so proud of them. Went on and on about how practical it is and how he couldn't wait to rearrange each section the next day."

"I'm pretty sure you won't have that problem when talking with Heath. He's a goofball. And I know you think he's cute."

I make eye contact with an elderly woman as we both reach for the same loaf of bread.

She's probably noticing the rush of color in my face.

I motion for her to take it as I pick up another one. I shift my phone to my other ear. "I mean, yeah, of course he's cute, Arry. I'd be dumb to say he's not."

"Then try one date and see how it goes."

"What if he doesn't even show up? His prank might be to

ditch me."

"Then you do something juvenile and stupid to get back at him. Circle of life, girl."

I smile at how Ariana's tone changed to a feisty queen bee. Part of her DOES believe that Heath could be messing with me.

I mean, obviously, I think. It's hard to not assume the worst when it comes to a guy like that.

"Well," I say, "I do kinda wanna see if he does the ditching and ghosting thing. It would prove that I'm right about him being like everyone else who trashed me along the way."

"You gotta relax and enjoy his company. He thinks you're awesome."

"But how can I get through a dinner if I'm on edge?"

"Talk about the basics. Shallow stuff. You'll avoid any turmoil that way."

"Arry—"

"Do it, Cassie. He'll pester me and Ian to be the liaisons for all eternity if you don't."

I slowly push my cart toward the shortest checkout line, accepting the high probability that it'll be the one line that doesn't move an inch for twenty minutes. "All right. One date. Only one. That should be enough to prove to everyone that we aren't ever going to be friends."

"Good luck. Have fun with him, Cass."

I hang up and begin setting my items on the conveyor belt. *What did I just set myself up for?*

A bag of yellow rice tips over and falls to the floor. I bend to pick it up, almost hitting my head on the magazine rack. My hands are shaking.

Have fun? I'll be a jittery, jumpy mess the whole time.

Five

Heath

I usually don't like to work Saturdays, but a couple of downtown businesses requested emergency cleaning for their sidewalks and storefronts. Word gets around that I am THE go-to person for all thorough sanitizing.

No one crushes the job like I do. Twenty cool guy points for me.

But the chores at home always come first. Ten seconds into cleaning the microwave and Ian's number pops up on my phone. I don't really want Diesel to hear the whole conversation if it's about Cassie, so I hold the phone to my ear and do my best to scrub with one hand. "Hey, what's up?"

"Heath, I had to spill your secret question to Ariana. She said you refused to tell her."

"Yeah, man, because I knew you would be the messenger. And when were you gonna tell me about Cassie being in the wedding?"

"Slipped my mind," Ian says. "But it's all good now, right? You got her number."

I glance back at Diesel. He's sitting at the kitchen table with headphones on, looking like he's concentrating on beating a record in one of his racing games. Even if he can't hear me, there's a chance he's turned the sound down and is covertly eavesdropping. Half his breakfast is still on the plate… the breakfast I worked so hard to make.

"I just called her," I tell Ian. "The conversation lasted maybe four minutes."

"Better than ten seconds, bud. The dog question didn't work?"

"It bought me some time. But I need her to see that I'm done with the pranks and trouble. I'm not who she thinks I am."

"Then you wait for her to make the next move. I bet Cassie wants to get revenge over lukewarm soup and breadsticks. She'll totally beat you up."

I roll my eyes at his mocking guffaw. "Nice pep talk, Ian. Later." I hang up and move on to scrubbing the kitchen sink.

Forced to wait for a call that realistically won't come has me feeling nothing but helpless. Even if I found Cassie's house and held up a handwritten sign professing how much she means to me… she'd still desire to see me pummeled to the ground instead of cuddling together on the couch with champagne, garlic toast, and a movie of her choosing.

Cassie Wicker. I need her… not want… need.

"Seriously," I say out loud, "this is one of the grossest messes I've cleaned up in the kitchen."

"Uh huh," Diesel says from behind the fridge door. "Where's the rest of the orange juice?"

I turn off the faucet and survey what's caked all over the

sink walls. Dried red sauce, cheese, several globs of green, and remnants of a catastrophic macaroni chicken salad from three nights ago. Glad it was me that got sick from it and not Diesel. Kid has the stomach of a Spartan.

"Dad?"

"What?"

"Orange juice. Thought we had some left."

"Yeah. Top shelf. Behind the milk."

"Oh. Yeah, there it is."

I watch Diesel pour himself a big glass and he downs it like he's been lost in the desert for three weeks.

"Dees, I gotta go to work in a few. You about ready to walk over to Ryan's house?"

"Yeah."

"Why didn't you eat the hash browns?"

"They're soggy."

I bring Diesel's plate of unfinished food to the sink, calculating which pieces I should drop in the disposal versus the trash or eating it myself. "I cooked them fine."

"No, they're disgusting."

"At least you ate everything else."

"You always ruin the pancakes, Dad. They tasted like burnt marshmallows."

I shrug, chuckling at his description. "Can't help you there. I love the charcoal taste."

"And THIS is why we buy microwaveable food." Diesel folds his arms while backing toward the living room. "Bye, Dad."

"Hey. You know I'm trying to keep us decently healthy, right?"

"You're still bad at cooking," he says. "But thanks anyway."

I know when Diesel's trying to be difficult just for the sake of it. I hear him muttering as he looks for his shoes and follow him to the door. "Diesel." I point at the shoe basket on the floor. "Right there, dude."

He quickly puts them on and looks me up and down as I stand between him and the front door. "What?"

"You're too much like me when I was a kid. I hope you don't talk to your teacher or to girls in that way."

"What way?" Diesel asks. "I'm just being honest, Dad."

"I'd prefer if you didn't say to my face that I suck at cooking. Raw honesty should be followed up with a compliment."

"I'll compliment you later," he says and dashes out the door.

There's always one more thing left to say when your kid leaves the house—I want to yell after him to stay on the sidewalk. But this time I don't. Diesel knows the safety rules. Kid's had them memorized since he was four.

The little smart-butt.

* * *

Doesn't matter if it's sweeping, shoveling, mopping, or scrubbing— I have an intense look on my face while working.

Penchant for perfection and all that.

I'm just starting to tackle a cluster of cobwebs in an antique store when my phone rings, and it takes me a minute to safely re-position on the ladder. I can't be more surprised at whose number it is… yet, it feels like destiny has already won.

"Cassie?"

"Okay, Heath," she grumbles on the other end.

"Okay what?"

"I'll go out with you."

The cobweb duster slips from my hand and clatters on the

floor. I mouth "sorry" to the employee who sternly eyeballs me as she walks past.

"So," I say to Cassie, "you're saying yes?"

"I am," Cassie says. "One date with you. That's it, Heath."

I climb down the ladder and stand against the window to let people pass by. "Are you still okay with dinner?"

"Sure."

Be cool, I think. *Be cool, Heath. Don't get too excited.* "Any place in mind?"

"Italian and Chinese are my favorites. But I love Mexican too. Or steaks."

"Thanks for narrowing it down, Cass," I say with a chuckle.

Cassie doesn't laugh. But she does choose a restaurant. "I'll meet you at Bella's Garden."

"I don't get to pick you up?"

"No. Meet me at seven tomorrow night."

"Will you at least let me pay for—"

Click.

Of course she hangs up on me again. Tricky woman.

But I know we can find common ground. There's always common ground.

* * *

The rest of Saturday rolls by slower than it ever has. My confidence is high right up until Sunday night when it takes a serious nosedive—an hour before I drive to the restaurant for my date with Cassie. Our first official date.

Haven't been hit with nerves this intense before.

And Diesel isn't helping much with his constant talking.

"Dad, if Cassie doesn't want the chocolates, can I have them?"

"What makes you think she won't?"

"What makes you think she will? She'll think they're fake or poisoned or something. You always played jokes on her."

I look back at Diesel, seeing him aggressively shake the box of chocolates. I take it from him, hugging it to my chest, and return to the closet. "I thought you were on my side, Dees."

"I am, but I don't think she'll eat the chocolate."

"It's supposed to be a peace offering. I'm sticking with it."

Diesel doesn't argue and I hear him bounce onto my bed. He's apparently making it his mission to drive me nuts. "Hey, dude," I say, "are you wearing my cologne?"

"Yeah."

"I should ask why but I won't." I step out of the closet and turn around so he can see my outfit. "What do you think of this? Blazer or no?"

"No. Too fancy." Diesel points behind me. "That one, Dad. Leather jacket over the light blue shirt."

"It's a little too warm tonight for leather."

"She'll think it looks good. You said all the girls loved when guys wore leather back then."

"Some. Not all."

"You gonna wear it or what?"

"I'll take your suggestion, Dees. Once."

Diesel high-fives me and goes back to gaming on his tablet. Then as I'm looking at myself in the full-length mirror, I hear him ask, "Where you taking Cassie?"

Man, this kid with the questions.

"I'm meeting her at that new place on Aspen Way."

"Bella's Garden?"

"You know it?"

"Yeah, that's the one that Mom kept talking about. She

wanted to go there with us when it opened."

That statement surprises me. Diesel didn't sound upset when he said it, but I look at him to see if he's harboring any strong emotion on his face. He's completely calm. "You remember that?" I ask.

"Yeah. But I'm not sad if you take Cassie there."

"Meeting her. I'm not taking her."

"But when do I get to meet her?"

"Not for awhile, my dude. She's kinda gun-shy."

"What's that mean?"

"My genius kid doesn't know the term 'gun-shy'? Shocker."

"But what's it mean?"

"It means that Cassie's distrusting and nervous about going out with me. I should be grateful at all that she agreed to it."

"That's facts, Dad."

"Facts," I echo, grinning at Diesel as he follows me into the living room. I stop at a mirror again to make sure every angle of my face and hair looks killer. "Is my hair too shiny?"

"No," Diesel says. "The gel's good. I wanna use some on my hair too."

"You can smolder it up tomorrow. Just don't be weirding out your babysitter with your sudden obsession with cologne and hair gel."

"But I'm not doing it to impress Fern, Dad. I'm practicing for a girl in my class. She always stares at me. And her smile is really cute."

"Dees," I chuckle. "For real?"

"Yeah. I'm never not serious about a cute girl."

"Is this what I get for being a troubled prankster all my life?" I put my hand on Diesel's shoulder as he looks up at me. "The sneakily-charming, genius-minded son of mine will charge around picking up girls better than me or my friends ever could?"

Diesel one-ups my smile with a bigger one of his own. "Yeah. Pretty much, Dad. But you just worry about getting Cassie."

"I'll do my best." I wait for Fern to make her way into the house before going to the garage. "Be good, Dees," I call out.

"You too, Dad!" Diesel yells back.

Supportive kid, I think. *A little too involved sometimes, but nothing better than having a kid who is encouraging me to get back in the dating game.*

Don't mess your chance up, Deitrich. Don't be stupid.

Six

Cassie

"Odessa, tell me if I'm crazy. I shouldn't be so paranoid, right?"

Odessa stares up at me, hoping I'll drop a marshmallow on the floor. It's risky pacing with a full bowl of Lucky Charms, but I can't sit without fidgeting. I have reasons to be nervous. But maybe those reasons aren't rational anymore.

Heath totally isn't gonna show up anyway. He so won't. Which means I'm allowed to be late or not even go.

"Just for kicks," I say to Odessa as she jumps on her bed with her bully stick, "I will go to the restaurant. Maybe I'll order myself dinner. Do some people watching."

Forget fancy clothes or perfume, I tell myself as I head out the door.

Simple black top and jeans with dusty boots. I'm not out to impress anyone.

* * *

Bella's Garden is one of those restaurants where couples tend to frequent when they are just past the honeymoon phase of their relationship. It's a little bit classy but also has the vibe of "I'm tired of the effort and just wanna eat bread and loaded potatoes without worrying about an attractive person's eyes on me".

I approach the entrance with all intention of sauntering in, expecting Heath to have ditched me in what I would call the typical form, and I know I'm going straight to the bar.

Sangria? No. Well... maybe. But I deserve something a bit stronger tonight.

I think about my choice of beverage while waiting for someone to give me the green light to seat myself, looking around at the current crowd and atmosphere. Fairly busy for a Sunday night. Lots of couples, a few tables of singles grouped together in a way that reminds me of high school science projects... and one guy sitting alone by the window.

OMG.

His back is to me, but there's no mistaking who it is. Heath showed up.

How?! Why? Ohmygosh. Ohhhhh no. Oh no... I'm not ready for this encounter.

Heath showed up to a real date at a real restaurant in a red carpet worthy outfit, gelled hair, and with what looks like a box of chocolates.

I can't do this.

Briefly making eye contact with a few people who are waiting for a table, I sprint back outside and vault into my car. I shut the door and slide down behind the wheel. My heart beats in my ears like a jackhammer on steroids, and I can't get a breath without sounding like an asthmatic.

Why can't I just face him? Why can't I just go on a stupid date with Heath Alun Deitrich?

Because, girl, my brain says, *he was your nightmare for four years.*

I sit slouched in my car in the parking lot with the radio as company for almost thirty minutes. The fear of Heath embarrassing me in front of a crowd of people is ever present even when I'm hiding.

I'm crazy, I tell myself. *I'm forty-one years old and crazy.*

Then I drive home.

* * *

I receive two texts from Heath at midnight—well after the planned date would've ended—and fight to ignore them.

HEATH: You ok, Cass?

HEATH: Will you call me?

Around 2 AM I eat two bowls of Trix on the couch, an episode of *Full House* playing on low volume in the background, and try to push down the guilt that is welling up inside me. If Heath really has changed his ways… then that means that I'M the jerk for ditching him.

I look at my phone and read the two texts again. Nothing says I have to text back and tell him that I'm fine. I don't need him to know my conflicting emotions.

A notification pops up in the corner of my phone's screen and it takes me a moment to realize what it is. Someone placed an order for cupcakes. I see their home address—not familiar with it. And then I see the name of the person who just made the order.

It's Heath. Heath just ordered two dozen chocolate caramel

cupcakes in the middle of the night.

What normal person does that?

Heath Alun Deitrich isn't just an annoying prankster.

Nope. He's insane.

Seven

Cassie

Not only am I exhausted from three hours of sleep, but I'm mad at myself for giving into the guilt. Here I am parked in front of my rival's house and going to his door with a bright red box of cupcakes that I spent the majority of the day making. It's four in the afternoon on Monday and I'm making amends for something I didn't think I would want to make amends for—ditching the guy who should've ditched me but made me nuts and made me the awful ditcher instead.

Heath's neighborhood looks very classic with all the white picket fences, high maintenance lawns, and extra spacious driveways. But I notice that his house is a single story unlike the tall, swanky homes around it. More of a humble exterior.

Humble home but a cocky attitude, I think.

I don't know how I'm supposed to smile or act chill when Heath comes to the door, but I don't have time to ponder my reaction. Within two seconds of ringing the doorbell, the front door opens. But it's not Heath standing there. It's his kid.

"Hi. I'm Diesel."

"Hi, Diesel. I'm Cassie." A smile lights my face without effort. Diesel is an adorable miniature version of his dad. And very gregarious for his age.

"Yeah, I know your name is Cassie," he says. "Did you really get my dad locked up in juvie?"

"Um. Well… not exactly. I sort of—"

"Oh, very actually, yes." Heath walks up behind Diesel, his hair a poufy mess which I take to mean that he probably just woke up from a nap. His cozy-looking red pullover and black sweatpants add to the whole 'worn out single dad' vibe. "Cassie did that exact thing to me, Dees."

"So she really is a hardcore tattletale," Diesel says, looking from me to his dad. "That's crazy."

Heath and I stare at each other, breathing softly, Diesel standing between us.

Awkward, I think. *Can't deny that. But, wow, does Heath look good in that outfit.*

"Here," I say. "You ordered these." I hold out the cupcake box for Heath to take.

"No." Heath scrunches his face, studying the box as if it was a mystical artifact. "I don't think so."

"Nope," Diesel says. "That was me." He grabs the box from my hands as I look at Heath in confusion. "I used Dad's credit card."

I watch Heath run a hand through his hair, biting his lip in a half-ashamed way and then I ask Diesel, "What'd you get the cupcakes for? Is it your birthday?"

"No." Diesel grins slyly with a wink and backs into the house with his score of chocolate caramel cupcakes.

Heath and I are left alone on the porch and I almost laugh. "Not only does he look like you, Heath, he acts like you too."

"I swear, Cassie, that's not his usual behavior. Well, the wink maybe. But the hijacking my credit card thing… I'll get him back for that."

"Sure you will." I take my glasses off to rub my eyes. "I really can't believe I drove fifteen minutes to put myself in this situation."

Heath leans against the doorframe and smiles, watching as I fix my bangs and put my glasses back on.

"And about last night," I say, "I'm sorry I left you hanging. Thing is, I got all this major baggage and emotional scars and I had parked my car and went into the restaurant and I saw you waiting for me. I freaked out. I ran back and sat in my car for twenty-five minutes trying to figure out why I couldn't just move past my paranoia. But the paranoia won."

"Not completely. You're standing here at my door with a nervous smile on your face. It's very cute."

YOU'RE very cute, Heath, I think. I scowl at myself for having that thought.

"Listen," I say, "I have conditions if you'd like to go out with me."

I had planned on jumping right into an intense spiel, figuring that Heath will question my reasoning for avoiding him. But he continues to look at me with playful eyes and a half-smile.

"Name them, Cassie," he says.

The tone of Heath's voice throws me off. It's like he wants me to ramble. But I don't know how comfortable I am setting up rules in front of a guy who never followed any to begin with.

I peer around him to see his living room, trying to seem casual. "Wow, I did not expect this level of order inside your house."

"I've had to be the one to keep things clean."

"Well, here is a fun fact for you, Heath," I say, ignoring the "Do Not Be Random" filter flashing in my brain, "I gotta tell you that my house is a disaster."

"Clutterbug?" he asks with that playful grin.

"Just disorganized. Trying to improve on it."

"I could help you."

"No thanks. Did you always imagine yourself to be a homemaking dad? Or was this just a way to keep your lover happy?"

"Cass." Heath's voice is serious now. His smile has faded. "I think you're trying to talk your way out of a date with me. Name the conditions and let's make this happen."

I back down the steps, glancing at the sidewalk. Heath follows me.

"Please, Cass."

I look up at him as I stand against my car. Heath leans in close and whispers, "Just tell me give me a shot."

"Here's the thing," I say, "I don't do dinner dates. I should've told you that before, but after the string of nightmare experiences I've had… I can't do anything at night. Has to be a morning date."

"No problem. I get up early."

"And also," I say, "no sitting on the same piece of furniture. No same couch or bench or booth. There has to be a gap."

"That's fine. Breakfast tomorrow then? Six-thirty at Cobalt's."

"All right." I get into my car, watching him study my every move. "See you tomorrow, Heath."

And he says with a smile, "I really look forward to it,

Shortbread."

Yeah sure, I think as I drive away. I look in my rearview mirror, seeing him standing in the road, looking like a border collie ready to chase down a ball.

Maybe this date won't be a nightmare. But Heath talking about anything meaningful? Can't imagine. Not in this life.

Eight

Heath

Diesel and I order pizza for dinner and we eat it on the couch in front of the TV. I stare at him for awhile, hoping he'll tell me why he pulled the credit card stunt. Nothing. Kid just wolfs down slice after slice of pepperoni pizza and remains glued to an episode of *Avatar: The Last Airbender.*

"This show came out when I was in my twenties," I say. "I wasn't a kid but I loved it."

"Yeah."

"Who's your favorite character?"

"Probably Zuko," Diesel says.

"Mine too." I grab one more piece of pizza and set the box on the floor. "Why did you order cupcakes at two in the morning?"

He doesn't answer me.

"Dees. Tell me why you did that."

After another minute of chewing his pizza, Diesel turns off the TV and looks me directly in the eyes. "Because we have to try harder, Dad. Cassie has to know that you aren't giving up on her."

"And you knew she would come to our house?"

"No," he says with a shrug. "I wasn't sure. But it worked."

"And I thank you for that, dude. But from now on, don't use my card without my permission. That made us both look like shysters."

"You should utilize my cleverness more often, Dad."

"Good point," I say with utmost sarcasm as I watch him take his plate to the sink. "I'll keep you in mind."

"I have a lot of good ideas."

"Appreciated. But I'm going out with Cassie tomorrow so I don't need any extra help."

"But if you do, Dad, I'm here."

"I know. You cool with Ryan's mom taking you to school tomorrow? Don't know if I'll make it back after breakfast to see you off."

"Yeah. And you don't need to ask Fern to come in the morning. I can take care of myself."

"I know you can take care of yourself. But I don't trust that you'll eat a balanced breakfast without an adult making it for you."

Diesel sighs and rolls his eyes. "Fine, Dad. But Fern has to make the bacon extra crispy."

I grin, glad to have dodged a ridiculous debate, and Diesel begrudgingly high-fives me.

Parenting for the win.

* * *

Cobalt's Diner. I'm excited when I arrive early and wait for Cassie—my favorite breakfast spot in town AND enjoying it with the woman of my dreams. I feel like jumping up and down like Diesel used to do when waiting in line for his favorite rollercoaster.

Cassie pulls into a parking space far from the diner and takes forever to get out of her car. I can tell that her outfit is meant to be very casual and is maybe meant to weird me out, but I honestly think she has never looked sexier—zero makeup, orange oversized sweatshirt, mermaid-blue leggings, tattered white Converse.

Ugh. The sweatshirt over the leggings is killing me. And her frizzy bangs. So cute.

"Morning, Cassie. Have you had your coffee yet?"

"Nope. And you're taking a risk by talking to me without it."

I try not to smile at her cranky voice but I'm tickled by it. "I'll try to avoid poking the bear. I need my coffee too."

"Not as bad as I do," Cassie says as she passes me through the door. "Black coffee is my oxygen."

I grin when I follow her inside, pausing to make sure the plastic-wrapped bouquet of flowers is still safe inside my coat. I'm thankful it's chilly this morning so that I have a reason to be wearing a few layers… and to be able to hide my daring romantic gesture.

Nine

Cassie

We sit at the counter and I automatically scoot over so that there are two stools between us. Heath moves to sit right beside me. Again I scoot to create a gap. We play the silly musical chairs game four more times until Heath bursts out laughing. "What are you doing, Cass?"

"Sorry." I force myself to stay put as he sits to the left of me. "Just a reflex."

"A reflex?"

"Sitting next to you brings up that old paranoid feeling."

"I'm not going to prank you." He winks at me before perusing the menu. "Promise."

Danger zone, I think. *I'm in the danger zone.*

Despite Heath and I having a few gray hairs and all the aches and pains of middle age, I'm remembering high school more clearly than ever.

"May I offer you a compliment?" Heath asks.

"Sure," I say.

"Your headband is adorable. And your perfume smells great."

I feel myself start to smile and hold the menu up to my face. "Thanks. Your cologne is quite strong."

"In a good or bad way?"

"It's good. You smell like citrus." I drop the menu when I hear coffee being poured into the mug in front of me and Heath chuckles at my expression. "That was fast," I say.

"Yeah. I just mouthed the word 'coffee' to the staff and they got right on it."

I roll my eyes, take a sip, and feel instant peace. "Just so you know, I will let you pay."

"Well, that's encouraging," he says brightly. "And by the way, my cologne is a blend of citrus, cedar, and eucalyptus. Interesting mix, right?"

"Sure." I glance at him before finalizing my decision on what I'm gonna order and we simultaneously flag the waitress down. I feel like I should be worried that I'm about to have a fake spider thrown at me or a water gun blasted in my eyes, but Heath just quietly sips his coffee and looks at me with a straight face as we wait for our food.

"So, Heath," I say, keeping my gaze on the salt shaker, "you're already training your son to pick up girls?"

Ten

Heath

"Why do you ask that?"

"When I met Diesel at your door yesterday he smelled like three hundred dollar cologne."

"He's learning that skill with minimal coaching. I was never a womanizer, Cassie."

"But why was he doused in cologne?"

"He has a crush. First one he's told me about. I'm just trying to be supportive." My attention diverts when our food arrives, and I reach past Cassie to grab the salt. I laugh when she flinches. "What's wrong?"

"Just… another reflex. History of being pranked."

"I can apologize countless times," I say, "but I doubt you will ever stop being jumpy."

"Well, anyway," Cassie says, eyeing me intensely as I salt my eggs, "Diesel's probably gonna steal hearts when he reaches high school. He's quite the schmoozer. And you're sure you never were a player?"

"I hardly had any girlfriends. I swear on that."

"Hm. Maybe that's because other girls thought you were gross too."

"Gross?" I shake my head with a half-smile as I cut into a stack of pancakes. "You can insult me better than that."

Cassie shrugs and starts meticulously cutting her bacon into tinier and tinier pieces. She shifts on her stool, turning her back to me as she mixes the microscopic bacon pieces in a pool of syrup and butter. "So, um, when did you stop wearing earrings?"

"Earrings?" I say, chuckling at the super shy way she had asked the question. I wait for her to look back at me.

"Yeah." She touches the rim of her glasses, her cheeks turning red, still not looking at me. She fiddles with a sugar packet. "The earrings you sported in eleventh and twelfth grade."

I lean in—so badly wishing I could give her a kiss—and fold my arms on the counter, grinning when she looks into my eyes. "Oh, Shortbread," I tease, "I never knew you were so turned on by the pirate look."

"No, it's not the pirate look. It's just... you know..." She scoots her stool away.

"You liked me."

"I didn't."

"You thought I was hot."

"No."

"Then the subconscious part of you did. And I think it's so cute that you admit that now. You liking my earrings, Shortbread."

"Well, it's not something I'm attracted to anymore." She straightens her shoulders and takes a bite of her waffle, trying to look the opposite of what her face is showing. "So not."

I bust up laughing, nearly falling off my stool. "Your face is so red, Cass. You loved my earrings and you thought I was crazy attractive."

Cassie coughs and I wonder if it's to disguise a laugh, but then she casually says, "Liking someone's appearance is not the same as liking their personality. I never liked your personality."

"Ouch." I grin as I drink more coffee. "That's a painful notion."

"Look, Heath, are we going to talk about anything serious? Like, maybe a conversation that doesn't involve making me blush?"

"Absolutely. I would like to know how the sassy Cassie from high school turned into a sporty adrenaline junkie."

"I'll tell you how." Cassie waves her fork in the air. "A nasty break-up. I craved fun challenges like intense trekking expeditions and skydiving every other weekend. That thrill-seeking phase started right after my first serious relationship's implosion."

"And how old were you then?"

"Twenty-two. The peak of my adventures was my early thirties. Slowed down pretty quick after that."

Slowed down? Not in the slightest, Cass, I think.

"Well, you've kept in really great shape."

"Thanks, Heath."

"You're welcome." I smile and take another bite of pancakes. "What else have you done that you haven't documented?"

"I documented pretty much all of it. Gonna be printing out all the photos soon to put into an album."

"You like old fashioned photo albums?"

"I'm big on having hard copies of everything. This digital age is creepy."

I nod. "I'm with you there. Diesel thinks my cassette tape collection is crazy old."

"Forty-one shouldn't feel that old. Kids remind us of how retro we are."

"Yeah, they do. Is that why you never had kids?"

"Because they make me feel ancient? No. I haven't had kids because I've not found a guy who has made me want to tie the knot and raise a family."

"Oh. Simple as that?"

"Simple as that. No right man out there."

"Crappy dating scene, huh?"

"Yeah. So much so that I've sworn off serious relationships."

"I noticed you haven't been as active on your public blog either. No new posts about epic bungee jumps, skydives, or mountain climbing. What is it? Boredom? A flatline in your list of goals?" I take a big gulp of coffee before adding, "Or is it a midlife crisis?"

Eleven

Cassie

Midlife crisis. One of the rare times I've actually heard that phrase uttered out loud by someone. Always sounds humorously cinematic for some reason.

Midlife crisis. I'm having a midlife crisis.

"That's one way to put it," I say. "Definitely feeling in a slump these days. Stuck."

"Me too. But seeing you after so long, Cassie… it really has stirred things up in me. I'm interested. Very interested in pursuing you."

"Heath Alun Deitrich," I say, secretly loving the sound of his full name, "what honestly compelled you to spring out of the woodwork after all these years and want to spend time with a woman who still resents her past with you?"

"Because you're cute. You're ambitious, sexy, feisty, a genuine sweetheart behind that cynical wall, and you're single."

His cocky grin weakens my inner defense system and I face

the coffee maker. "You make me nervous."

"I don't mean to," Heath says.

There's a nagging, complicated transparency flickering between us. Driving my heart and brain crazy.

I look down at where my purse is next to my feet and slide off the stool to pick it up. I pull out the mangled notebook I used to carry around every single day of tenth grade. "I'm open to spending more time with you, Heath, as long as you do something for me."

"Anything." Heath talks around a bite of gelatinous scrambled eggs. "You name it."

"There will be parameters."

"Understood. But didn't you already state your conditions for us hanging out?"

"This is different. I want to put high school behind us."

"It is behind us. I just want to have a chance to get to know you as who you are today, Cass. And for you to know me."

I hesitate before revealing the notebook to Heath, clutching it in my lap. "We should air out all our past grievances."

"Grievances." He smirks at the word. "And that's gonna help us get closer?"

"No. But it'll ease the tension I feel when I'm around you."

"All right. You first."

The nonchalance in his voice suddenly puts me into a state of annoyance again and I slam the notebook down in front of him, flipping to the third page. "Here."

Heath looks from me to the notebook, perplexed by the frown on my face. "What's this?"

"Read it," I say. "It's all the bad and humiliating incidents from high school. I kept a record."

He looks like he's about to smile and not take me seriously, but as soon as I set my coffee down and fold my arms with an icy stare, he picks up the notebook and starts reading.

The guy is silent reading. S-l-o-w-l-y.

Watching him take forever to get through the top half of the page plunges me into aggravation and I can't stop myself from telling him all what I've been holding back.

I wanna pick a fight. I shouldn't. But I never got to do it back then. I never got that final confrontation.

"You know, Heath, you never asked me a single question in high school. All I heard from your mouth were immature comments after you carried out each prank."

"Yes, I was immature. So were you. Your immaturity just happened to be layered beneath the good grades, perfect attendance, and the 'I'm a sassy teacher's pet and I know it!' vibe."

"I was not sassy. I wasn't popular either. The cheerleaders picked on me like crazy—they spread all those rumors about us being a couple after the cafeteria incident."

"Rumors mean nothing. I never even heard about those. But if I had heard it…" He grins. "I would've wanted the rumors to be true."

"Read this one aloud," I say, pointing at a sentence in the middle of the page.

"I would love to, Shortbread, but your handwriting is awful."

I growl at his wink and slide the notebook back toward myself. "Okay. I'll tell you. Remember PE?"

"Of course I do. I did some of my best work during that period."

"Well, do you remember the day I sprained my ankle?"

"No."

"You flicked a giant beetle on my face that time we were both in the outfield."

Heath crosses his arms, looking at me with defensive eyes. He responds so fast that I know he remembers all the incidents as vividly as I do. "The beetle was an accident, Cass. It startled me when it landed on my hand."

"You should've just killed it."

"The flick was a reflex. I couldn't help it."

"It was stuck in my hair for ten minutes, Heath! I ran around screaming and swishing my hair trying to get it out and then twisted my ankle in a gopher hole."

Heath smirks and reaches for his coffee. "What about when you vomited on me at the end of that two mile run?"

I slide off my stool. Can't go over all this when I'm sitting down.

Time to flail and bounce around in an exasperated manner.

"So what, Heath? You sprayed yourself off with the hose."

"My mom couldn't get the smell out of my shirt. I had to toss it."

"That incident was your own fault," I say.

"How so?"

"I didn't eat lunch that day because I was too nervous for my math test, but then I felt light-headed before PE so I asked Ariana if she had an extra snack and she gave me half of a tuna sandwich."

Heath turns to watch me pace. "But where do I come in?"

"Ariana waited two years after graduation to tell me that she had gotten that sandwich from Ian who got it from you, Heath. Your mom had packed it and Ian had eaten one half of it and he didn't want the rest so he gave it to Ariana. She gave it to me saying she had packed it for herself. So... I trusted it."

"So what? I didn't make the sandwich."

"But you knew it was bad tuna. And you gave it to Ian."

"True, Shortbread. It was bad tuna. But you could've aimed your vomit spray in a different direction instead of directly on me."

"I didn't want to."

"Why?"

"Because, Heath, that vomiting incident was two weeks after you got me put in detention."

"Refresh my memory of how I did that," he says.

I groan at his relaxed tone and how he is just sitting back and enjoying my caffeine-fueled rant.

"Well, it's like this," I say, spitting it all out in one long breath, "you got into my locker with the help of one of the cheerleaders and filled my back-up water bottle with vodka. And although it was the cheerleader who told the principal, you were the one who brought in the alcohol. Apparently you did this because you were getting back at me for the one prank I victoriously pulled on you."

"You pulled a prank on me?" he asks. He sounds more confused this time and incredibly eager to know the details. "When was that?"

"Yes. It was the only time I had the nerve to participate in your shenanigans."

"And? What'd you do? I don't remember this."

I can hear snickers and whispers behind me and become keenly aware that other people in the diner are now engrossed in my animated story time. Heath is locked in on me, eyes intense as he waits for me to continue.

"This is what happened," I say. "You always kept a bottle of hair gel in your locker. I got Ariana to stand guard while I swapped your gel with orange juice and vodka. For some dumb reason you decided to go to town with gel that day and tipped the bottle straight onto your head and were doused in it. I saw the whole thing from further down the row of lockers and would've danced in celebration, but I ended up turning and getting a classroom door slammed in my face. Busted nose."

I see pure amusement in Heath's eyes and his struggle to avoid exploding in laughter. He turns away with his just-refilled mug of coffee as I keep looking at him, and he takes a sip while looking in a completely different direction. I bite my lip—afraid to laugh at my own expense and afraid to let Heath see that he's finally got me laughing with him—but I can't contain the giggles.

Heath faces me and starts to say something before snort-laughing into his coffee. He spits a mouthful out on the counter, immediately covers his mouth, and looks at me with wide eyes. We both fall apart in boisterous, childish laughter.

Twelve

Heath

I haven't laughed that hard with anyone in a long time. Cassie's way of telling a story in an increasingly angry voice coupled with her spastic arm gestures is another level of cute and hilarious. I watch her try to resume a serious coffee-drinking mode and then see her begin lining up a sugar packet, napkin, and a stray dime on the counter. "Um, what are you doing, Cass?"

"Figuring out what I'm taking home."

"What for?"

"On every date I go on I take one thing from it to remind me of the experience. It can be a straw wrapper, sugar packet, movie ticket stub, or menu. I have two scrapbooks full of it."

"All your dates?"

"Yeah. Tangible memories. It also counted when I would go on dates with a serious boyfriend. Every time I went out, I brought something small back with me."

That's quite a quirk, I think. *Too cute for words.*

"Cass," I say as we make our way toward the door, "I actually do have something for you."

She stops, looking at me as I reach into my coat, and tilts her head when she sees the flowers. "Are those dahlias?"

"Yeah." I hold the bouquet out to her. "Here."

"Where's the prank?"

"There is none. You deserve flowers, Cass. You've always deserved them."

She is still looking suspicious as she takes them, but she smiles as we exit the diner. "I can't put these in a scrapbook."

"No, but I think it's time you upgraded your 'I-went-on-a-date' souvenirs to ones that you can display on a shelf."

She stares at the flowers as she walks along, meeting my eyes when she notices that I'm following her to her car. "Thank you. They're… they're very pretty."

"Anytime, Cass. Can we meet up here again tomorrow?"

"Well…"

"We could pick a different place if you want. Or go for a walk or something."

"I'm going on a run tomorrow morning. Not planning on breaking that routine."

"Okay," I say, leaning against her car with the confidence of a high school football star. "Then I'll run with you."

"You like running?"

"I'll run if it means I get to hear more about your incident list and anything else you have to spill."

Cassie shakes her head with a smile. "The park on Wilson Street. Been to that one?"

"I have," I say.

"I run around it several times to mark three miles."

"I'm there."

Cassie gets into her car and watches me back away. "Snake-bait," she says out her window, "I won't slow down for you."

"I'll keep up, Shortbread."

This date went so well, I happily think to myself. *She showed up and I got her to laugh. Best feeling ever.*

Thirteen

Cassie

I'm imbued with a false sense of security I've felt before around other guys. Heath's showing a sweet side I did not ever see in high school AND he is funny—his facial expressions are so entertaining.

My sense of humor was sorely lacking back then, I think. *I'm dumb to not have ever found Heath funny before.*

Either I've got good reason to have butterflies in my chest, or Heath is doing what ninety-seven percent of guys have done to me. They treat me like the queen of the world with a sexy charm, turn me into a puddle with their dreamy eyes, and then stomp on my heart with no remorse like a boneheaded jackass.

I have to find out if he's really into me for the right reasons and not here to just bust me up like a train smashing a car on the tracks. I'm taking a risk by allowing him to join me in my sacred running time which I always have done alone.

Keep your distance, Cassie, I tell myself. *Don't fall for the deceivingly sugary game tactics.*

* * *

Heath shows up to the park the following morning at the same time as I do. He's wearing an off-white hoodie and legitimate gym shorts.

Man, his legs look good.

But I don't know if I like sensing a friendly competition about to happen—he was a taunting monster when we ran laps in PE while I always came in last.

"Like what you see, Shortbread?"

I turn away at his teasing question, clearing my throat as I drop into a stretch. "I assume you have a treadmill."

"I do." He comes around to face me. "And a few weights. I try to do a short workout each night."

I should've worn a looser fitting t-shirt, I think. *The way he's looking at me right now is making me incredibly self-conscious. I'm not sixteen! I'm forty-one! Heath, augh! Why do you have to have eyes the color of a crystal blue lake?*

"Can we call this a date too, Cass? You and me running together?"

"Sure." I get busy untangling the earbud cord from around my phone. "Whatever you wanna call it. But if you don't mind, I have to run the first mile to my music to get in the zone. Just give me space for a few minutes."

"What you listening to?"

"You don't have to know every detail about me, Heath. I can keep some things private."

"Are you ashamed of your music choices?"

"No, it's just that it's my disjointed playlist and I don't want it suddenly skipping to a song that's embarrassing."

"What's an embarrassing song that you like?"

"Forget it."

"C'mon. Let me listen."

"No way."

"Okay, I wanna hear it even more now." He reaches for my phone as I hold it tight to my chest.

"Heath, no."

"Just give me an earbud, Cass."

"No. Get your own music."

"Just one song!" Heath shouts like a little kid on Christmas. He starts to wrap his arms around me from behind and I completely panic, loosening my grip on my phone. Heath swipes it, putting the earbuds in as he runs away.

"Hey! You got Blink-182 on here!" he says between breaths.

"Heath, give me my phone!"

For a few brief moments as I chase after Heath, I picture us both as our teenage selves in PE—myself having clumsy strides and Heath with his rocker hair and gazelle-like speed.

"Heath, give it back!"

"Catch up, Shortbread!"

I grumble to myself, thinking twice about going for a jump and tackle.

We aren't young anymore. A move like that would be painful.

I slow to a walk and watch Heath look back at me with disappointment in his eyes.

"Hate to ruin your fun, Heath," I say, "but I don't want to injure myself."

"Fair. But I love it—you running after me like old times." He holds my phone above his head and looks ready to chuck it hard like he's throwing a football, but instead half-smiles and waits for me to approach. He gently tosses it to me.

"Sorry, Cass. Couldn't help myself. You've always been great fun to mess with."

"That's very flattering," I say. "You gonna run alongside me for real now or take my phone again?"

"I won't. If it makes you feel better about my shenanigans though, tell me another incident. That's why we're out here together in the first place, right? To discuss the history."

"It is. Do you remember the squirt gun?" I ask as we start running.

"The one during assemblies?"

"Yes."

Heath chuckles. "I'll be honest, Cass, I loved doing that to you."

"But you brought that thing every single assembly. Always found a way to sit right behind me. I thought at some point you would get bored of it."

"Your hair looked so sexy when it got wet. Plus, I loved how you always snarled at me before moving to a different seat."

"Yeah. I moved," I say, rolling my eyes at his smirk. "And you always followed. I felt that dumb splash of water on the back of my head ten seconds later."

Heath starts running backward, grinning at me. "It was fun," he says. "And your reaction was hysterical."

"Uh huh. And what about the exploding soda incident? Remember that one?"

"Sort of. But I thought Ian was partly to blame for that."

"That was all you, Snakebait," I say.

"Really?"

"Yes. And here's how it went down—Ian owed me a soda because I helped him pass all of his vocabulary tests for a month, somehow you ended up with the can he was going to give me, and of course, I should've known… you shook that soda to death before slyly handing it to me and I opened it like an idiot. It exploded all over my math homework and textbooks, AND the inside of my locker was sticky for weeks!"

"Yeah, okay," Heath says, chuckling, "because a normal person would've popped a soda while standing at their open locker."

Easing from a full run to a fast walk, I check my current heart rate and turn to go the opposite way on the path. "Listen, Heath," I say, "I had reasons for keeping my locker open when I ate snacks."

"Yeah? And why was that?"

"Because I liked using my locker as a place to write last minute notes."

"But it's not like you can sit in your locker and use it a secret hideaway."

"I know," I say. "I just liked the feeling I had when standing with it open and writing things down against one of the doors. And I had a ton of stickers inside it and I always added new ones. Almost every other day I had a new sticker to put in it."

Heath briefly passes me up as he says, "Huh. Stickers on locker doors. Never understood that one."

"Yeah. Because guys didn't do that," I say.

"I had one sticker in a binder though, Cass."

"Of what?"

"A motorcycle. Everyone thought I should've had one back then because of my obsession with leather and long hair, but I—"

"And your earrings," I interject.

"Yeah. My earrings. But anyway, I put a motorcycle sticker in my binder to remind myself that I needed to step up my badass image."

"But you never got a motorcycle. Not that I knew of."

"I know," he says. "I didn't get one. And I never got into drugs as everyone expected me to do."

I pause at a bench, bending to stretch and retie my right shoe. "That's good to know, Heath. Glad you didn't completely fall into the vat of peer pressure."

"A vat of peer pressure," Heath says with a laugh. "That's a good one, Cass. And hey, I got a fun, spontaneous question for you."

"Yeah?"

"Yeah. It's a question to help me learn about the current you. What's your go-to comfort movie?"

I straighten my back, glancing toward the parking lot. "You assume that everyone has a comfort movie?"

"Yep."

"So is this the start of a rapid-fire question segment in our reconnecting timeline?"

"Sure," Heath says. "Get to know each other on all levels. Go on. Favorite comfort movie."

I get back into my run and say over my shoulder, "*Say Anything.*"

"What's the reason for that?" Heath asks. He's breathing harder now.

"No reason other than John Cusack," I say.

"It's the young John Cusack, isn't it? That's what you like."

I look at him, see his toothy grin and raised eyebrows, and give an exaggerated shrug. "I like him in anything. Doesn't matter if he's old or young. *Serendipity* is another fantastic movie of his."

Heath snort-laughs. "You have goofy starry eyes, Cass.

Should I stop you before you get on a roll listing every single one of his movies?"

"I like a lot of actors. I'm sure you have your celebrity crushes too."

"Yeah, but none I've liked can compare to your beauty and amazing personality."

"Goodness, Heath." I roll my eyes. "Don't be putting me on that sort of pedestal."

"I'm not. Telling it like it is."

"Okay, well, what's your go-to comfort movie?"

"*Smokey And The Bandit*," he says.

"Never seen it."

"Are you kidding me?!"

"Nope."

"My dad introduced it to me when I was seven and it was the only thing we ever laughed at together. Watched it six times a year until I was about fifteen."

I slow to a walk again to catch my breath. "Must be very funny."

"It is. We should watch it sometime."

"Yeah, maybe," I say.

Heath follows me when I start heading to the parking lot. "Who's your favorite superhero, Cass?"

"Batman."

"Okay. Tell me why."

"I have to a reason to like him?"

"Yes. You can't just say your favorite superhero without a reason why."

"Is that a rule?"

"I made the rule up," Heath says.

I laugh at his bluntness. "Okay. I like him because I love the whole backstory and the comics and I just think Batman is the definition of cool."

"And what do you think of Iron Man?"

"He's awesome. The movie is fantastic too. The first one."

"Agreed. Diesel loves that movie too."

While grabbing a water bottle from the backseat of my car, I watch Heath get his own water out and come back toward me. He stands in one spot, observing as I do my post-run stretching.

"Shortbread, I'd like to propose that we keep having regular dates just like this. I don't mean to stifle you at all, but you and I are freelancers, so I know you have the time."

"I already mentioned yesterday that I'm open to more time with you," I say. "Just hope we can stay civil even when I bring up our past."

"Works for me," he says.

I study his face, curious as to why it is me out of all the women in the world that he has chosen to obsess over. "Am I that intriguing to you, Heath?"

"Yes."

"Even the grumpy and whiny parts?"

"Yes."

"Okay then. We continue regular dates."

"Can we hug to confirm the deal?"

"No."

"Handshake?"

"Nope. No purposeful physical contact."

"All right. Let's salute each other. Make the deal official."

I give a full body sigh and roll my eyes as we trade salutes. "You really turned into a dork, Heath."

"Yep," he says cheerfully. "That happened a few months into me becoming a dad. Rite of passage."

I half-smile, then look past him to watch a family out on a walk. Two elementary aged kids are holding the leashes of three Dalmatian puppies, while the mom and dad are making googly eyes at each other. It's a cute scene—almost makes me think I should get married and have kids.

"Cassie? What are you looking at?"

I jolt back to Heath. He takes a drink of water and looks around, wiping sweat from his forehead.

Wow, I think, *there's always something ridiculously gorgeous about a man with sweat glistening in his hair.*

"Before you go," Heath says, "do you need a souvenir to remember this date?"

"Nah, I don't have to cling to that silly tradition. The flowers you gave me yesterday were beautiful, but you don't have to keep gifting me things."

"How about if I supply you with tangible souvenirs on the days we go to the diner, and then on days where we meet up outside for runs or walks or whatever, we can make a memory in another way?"

"In what way?" I get nervous when he takes out his phone and duck down when he tries to put his arm around me. "What are you trying to do, Heath?"

"Nothing bad. I just..." He backs away, looking sheepish. "Can we take a picture together?"

"Keep distance," I say. "No arm around me or touching my hair or—"

"Okay, okay," he laughs. "It'll be candid. Don't even look into the camera if you don't want to. Act like you think I'm gross."

He takes his phone out and extends his arm as far as he can, making sure both of our faces are in the picture.

"I'll text it to you," he says after he takes it.

And not even ten seconds after driving from the parking lot, I hear my phone beep. I pull over to avoid an accident amidst my anxious curiosity.

Heath sent me the picture, and I'm amazed at how much I actually like it.

Fourteen

Heath

Cassie kicks off our next breakfast date by telling me about the "gluey binder" incident as she takes small bites of plain oatmeal. Surprises me that she would eat such a thing. Doesn't seem like an oatmeal kind of girl.

I take a bite of my corned beef hash, and in realizing how extra delicious it is, I offer some to Cassie.

"Cass, try this."

Cassie gives me a disgusted look as she flips to the next page in her notebook. "Are you serious?"

I smirk at her little snarl. "Just bite it off the fork."

"I'm not your girlfriend."

"Casual friends can share food too." I hold the fork aloft, glancing at the waitress when I hear her chuckling at our conversation. "C'mon. It's really good."

Cassie sighs. "You won't pull it away really fast or fling it on my head?"

"I won't. Promise."

"Okay."

Cassie tentatively accepts the forkful of food, and I can't keep from smiling when she meets my eyes in the middle of putting her mouth on my fork.

"Not bad," she says after she chews it. "But I could've taken some off your plate with my own fork too."

"Yeah," I say, "but that was cute. We need to build cute moments between us."

"Psh. Cute moments. Can I finish the story now about what you did to my binder?"

I nod as I sip my iced coffee. "I know what I did. I glued it shut."

"But how did you do that without me noticing, Heath? I thought I always had that binder with me."

"Oh," I say, "I distracted you with a fake tarantula. You dropped your messenger bag and ran screaming."

Cassie sighs and rolls her eyes at me. "I think I blocked the spider part out of that one."

"Probably. But anyway, I got access to the stuff in your bag. And by the way, Cass, you always overpacked it."

She shakes her head with a smile and looks back at the notebook. She doesn't say much else until I hear her mumble, "Can you still breakdance?"

I laugh. "When did you see me breakdance?"

"Twelfth grade. It was a football game and you and Ian danced right into the middle of the cheerleaders." She grins, and her cheeks flush. "They were so mad at you guys. But I'd say seventy percent of the crowd loved your moves."

"Including you, Shortbread?"

"Maybe."

"Uh huh, yeah," I say, wanting to keep her blushing, "you totally did."

"Well, what can I say, Snakebait, it was very smooth dancing. It was… sexy."

"Too bad I don't dance as often in public anymore," I say. I look to see if she is disappointed to hear that and smile to myself when I see her slight pouty face. "That was just a spur of the moment thing as most high school stunts are."

"Yeah, too bad." Cassie puts an elbow on the counter and closes the notebook. She points to the bag at my feet. "What's that? Are you trying to one-up your previous diner date souvenir?"

I grin at the eagerness in her voice. "You think I brought more flowers?"

"No, but I want to know if I should brace for confetti or something awfully sticky to fly out of it."

"Funny, Cass. No, it's something very cute." I bend down to pick the bag up and reveal the gift for her—a cartoony plush fox that just so happens to be wearing plastic glasses.

Cassie tilts her head as she takes it and she gingerly hugs it to her chest before setting it on the counter.

"I don't remember when exactly," I say, "but at some point in high school I overheard you excitedly screeching to someone that red foxes were your favorite animal. I wrote that tidbit of information down on the back of the algebra homework that I forgot to turn in."

"It's adorable."

"Yeah. His glasses even match yours." I gesture to the toy fox's red-rimmed glasses and then gesture to hers.

And YOU are the most adorable one, Cass, I think while smiling back at her.

Fifteen

Cassie

"Good morning, my Sassy Vocab Cassie," Heath quips on our second running date. "It's pretty cold so I got us some mochas. They'll stay warm in my car until we're ready to drink 'em."

"Do not call me 'Sassy Vocab Cassie'," I say. "Why do you even have to include the word 'vocab' in a nickname?"

"Because outside of you being 'Shortbread', Cass, you were the champion of spelling and complex word definitions in our class."

"What a weird thing to be nicknamed for. I feel like I should have a secondary nickname for you then."

"Like what?"

"Maybe something like 'The Rogue Bandicoot' or 'Mister Slick And Sly'." I look at him, stifling my own laugh when he cracks up. "It's stupid, I know, Heath. I can't think of anything creative right now."

"It's just fun to be weird with you," Heath says as he follows me into my run. "Really fun."

"Well, how's this for fun," I say. "Remember the incident with the bucket of water?"

"Oh yeah!" He grins as he keeps pace with me. "I'm still in awe that it actually worked on you, Cass. Bucket of water dumped on your head. Classic."

"I was dressed up for a group presentation. I didn't have time to change before I had to stand up there all dripping wet in front of everybody. And in a white blouse of all things!"

"For real," Heath says and laughs. "I'm surprised they didn't make you go to the principal's office to change. That shirt looked so tight and provocative on you."

"Because of the water, Heath! Once again, your doing."

"Apologies, Cass. But you know I couldn't resist the water pranks."

I roll my eyes as I speed up.

"Hey," Heath says, "let me take a picture with us in motion. Act like you're about to charge across a battlefield with epic music blasting around you."

"Seriously?" I say with a smirk.

"Seriously." He holds his phone above our heads. "Pose, Shortbread!"

Oh my gosh, I think when I see the picture. Our faces are semi-blurred and my hair is wild and covering my eyes. I look pissed in it and Heath has his mouth open in a very ridiculously overachiever smile.

"I guess we can call that a half cinematic and half awful picture," I say.

"Nothing awful about it," Heath says cheerfully. "Blurry pictures are fun."

I spit out a laugh. "Who in their right mind likes blurry

pictures?"

"I think it's artistic."

"Artistic?"

"Yeah," Heath says, "I've never been artistic really in anything but growing up people said they liked my flair behind the camera."

"I didn't know you liked taking pictures so much."

"I do. It's the best way to preserve fleeting moments." He grins and points toward his car. "Feel like one of those mochas, now, Cass?"

"Sure," I say.

Heath extends an offer for me to sit in his car with him, but I decline it, instead drinking my mocha while walking in a circle with my earbuds in. I know Heath is watching me and that he's silently laughing at my stubbornness, but I still don't want to be squished close to him.

Sitting in a guy's car... that's always a no.

But Heath contentedly perches himself on the hood of his car and just enjoys his view—which is me.

Sixteen

Heath

Cassie and I end up ordering the same breakfast on our third date to the diner. She surprises me by not rescinding on her order after I say mine, and then calls me a copycat in what sounds like a mix of a teasing and sultry whisper.

"You're the copycat," I say, lightly poking her shoulder with my fork. "I'm never such a thing."

"Oh, c'mon." She simultaneously shakes her head at me and smiles at the waitress when we get our plates of French toast and poached eggs. "I bet you copied at least two dozen tests in school, Heath."

"Um, more like four or five. I wasn't a prolific cheater, Cass. Even when I cheated I still managed to flunk them."

"Did you ever get detention because of that?"

"Because of cheating on a test? Not that I can remember."

"But you did rack up the most hours in detention out of anyone in our class." She smirks at me before sipping her coffee.

"It's amazing that you didn't get into some kind of record book for that."

I half-smile, completely charmed by her manner of flirting. "Speaking of detention," I say, "do you happen to like *The Breakfast Club?*"

"I haven't met anyone who doesn't like it."

"Then I have something that will surely excite you, Short-bread."

"Show me," she says.

I slowly reveal the poster from behind my back, letting her be the one to unroll it and discover what it is.

"Whoa, what?"

I laugh at the shriek in her voice.

"Heath, no way. Where'd you get this from?"

"It's great, right? Autographed poster of that movie."

"This is crazy. It's legit."

"It is, Cass."

"But you didn't tell me where it came from."

"Mr. Birdwell," I say.

"Who?"

"He's this eccentric old neighbor of mine who has these epic garage sales every week. Sometimes twice a week. His daughter helps him arrange the items he wants to sell and often sits outside on his driveway with him."

"And he sells stuff like this?" she asks, holding the poster up.

"Yeah. Almost all of it is vintage or retro. I love showing up just to talk to him because he has been so sweet to me and Diesel."

"But why doesn't he just have one giant sale and get rid of all his hoard at once?"

"He isn't a hoarder, Cass. And I don't know why he chooses

to sell his stuff in small batches versus all at once. That's just one of his quirks."

"And you've bought other things from him?"

"All the time," I say. "I find rare comic books, signed memorabilia from a variety of old school celebrities, and so many random things related to old movies and TV shows."

"This Mr. Birdwell sounds like my kind of friend."

"Yeah?"

"Yeah. When is his next garage sale?"

I keep her in suspense, downing the last of my iced coffee, and fold my arms on the counter with a smile. "Tomorrow," I say. "Wanna go with me?"

"I do," she says. "It's kinda been annoying to not have any friends that like vintage things like I do. Garage sales used to be my favorite way to get out in the neighborhood and be social."

"Well, Cass, now you have a garage sale buddy. And I'm proud to be a garage sale frequenter even if people think it's odd."

"I think it's cute," she says. "Matches your phase of life."

"Meaning what?" I ask with a wink. "You and I are both in similar phases… except your kid is a furball."

Cassie laughs. "This is true."

Total dog mom energy, I think as a gaze into Cassie's happy eyes, *and total girlfriend energy.*

Seventeen

$$Cassie$$

I park in front of Heath's house, seeing him patiently waiting for me outside his front door. He really doesn't have to be such a gentleman, but I choose not to make a fuss about it.

"Which way is Mr. Birdwell's house?"

"Left," Heath says as he joins me on the sidewalk. "He never has that many people swarming his sales, but it's amazing how he puts out so much stuff every single time."

"And you said his daughter helps him set it up?"

"Yeah. She's sits out there with him because she worries about his memory. But let me tell you, Cass, the man really zips around with his walker. He can be as loud and lively as a superstar comedian."

I giggle at Heath's description, not entirely believing it. "What's his first name?"

"Peider. But I rarely call him that. He loves hearing people use his last name, and I think it's because he thinks it sounds funny."

"Birdwell," I say to myself. "Yeah, it does sound kinda funny."

We reach the driveway of a very mellow yellow-painted house and I get my first glimpse of Mr. Birdwell. He's clean-shaven, hunched with a walker, got a few tufts of white hair on the top of his head, and he's wearing a massive grin while gesturing for anyone walking on the sidewalk to check out his sale.

"Hey, Birdwell," Heath calls out.

Mr. Birdwell takes a moment to turn and notice us. He pushes his walker along with one hand, waving with the other.

"How's it going, Heath? Where's Diesel? In school?"

"He is, yeah," Heath says. He trades boyish fist bumps with Mr. Birdwell. "I want to introduce you to a friend of mine."

"Oh yeah? You gonna buy something today?"

"I might. I'll have a look around." Heath then motions for me to move in and says, "Birdwell, this is Cassie. She wanted to come see your garage sale."

"Oh, Cassie!" Mr. Birdwell chirps with a bright smile, acting like he's known me forever.

I expect a simple handshake from him, but he leans in and gives me a hard embrace. "It's so nice to meet you," he says to me. "How long you been friends with Heath? You a new girlfriend?"

I hear Heath chuckling as I'm trapped in the hug with Mr. Birdwell. But I'm actually happy to be hugging this old gentleman... makes me feel like long lost family.

"Just an old friend of his," I say. "We're getting reacquainted."

"Well, that's good." Mr. Birdwell steps back from me and gestures to his garage. "Go on and look for treasures, Cassie. I'm sure you'll discover something special."

I hold in a laugh, enjoying his exuberant character. "Thank you, Mr. Birdwell. I'm sure I will."

Finally free to survey the sale without distraction, I meander around the tables, curious of the many many boxes, crates, and stacks of old books.

When I hear an especially zany laugh, I quickly look toward Heath and see that he's entertaining Mr. Birdwell with some silly story about Diesel.

Watching him interact with Mr. Birdwell and a few other neighbors in such a lovable, friendly manner brings up a random array of questions in my mind. Very serious questions about Heath's life that only just now do I badly want to know the answers to.

"Hey, Heath," I say, leaning in next to him as he carefully inspects a stack of Superman comic books, "why didn't I ever see your parents at any school functions? I think I knew and talked to all our other classmates' parents except yours."

Heath answers without pause. "Because I rarely saw my parents at home. They practically left me to raise myself."

"Why? What were they doing?"

"Drinking, snorting, dealing. Every unhealthy thing you can think of. And when they were home and heard about the things I had been up to…" He shrugs. "Consequences. Violent consequences."

"They hit you," I say.

"Sometimes. Or cut me with glass. I spent a lot of nights sleeping under park benches."

"I hate to hear that."

"I know. And I heard how loving your family was. Always was a little jealous of you for that."

"Sorry. Sorry to bring it up if it still hurts you."

"It's all good now, Cass."

Heath picks out a specific comic, presses it to his chest, and kneels down to rummage through a blue plastic box that's full of vintage *Star Trek* toys.

I love the look of intense concentration on his face and the way he is more determined to find a treasure than I am.

He briefly looks up and gives me a little smile and wink which takes me by surprise. My heart pounds as I pretend to smooth my hair.

"Heath," I say, "what about your girlfriend? Did she make you feel happy and safe?"

"You're asking about Diesel's mom?"

"I am."

"Yeah," Heath says. "She was amazing for a time."

"What was her name?"

"Lola."

I smile. "Like the bunny."

"Yeah. Like the bunny." Heath stands and moves to a bucket overflowing with rolled up movie posters. "She was a big time smoker and it got worse after having Diesel. She wouldn't give up the cigarettes even for him."

I follow him, looking back to where Mr. Birdwell is having a very spirited chat with another neighbor. "But you loved her anyway, didn't you?"

"We were an on and off couple for a long time. Did what I had to for our little family."

"Well, it looks like you're doing okay without her," I say.

"Mostly, yes."

I pick up a Wonder Woman t-shirt and check out both the front and back of it before setting it back on the table. "And how has Diesel handled the loss?"

"He had nightmares for three weeks straight after his mom's passing. Rough nights for both of us. But we're buddies. Got through it."

"That's good." I trade smiles with Heath as he points to Mr. Birdwell. "You going to tell another funny story to him?"

"Just gonna buy this comic and give him a hug. The guy loves to dole out bear hugs like they're the law."

I think of the big embrace that I got from Mr. Birdwell and have to agree. "He is a good hugger," I say.

"Oh, yeah. And I'd be in trouble if I walked away without one. It's part of his creed."

I laugh as I walk after Heath. "Okay, but before we finish up here, Heath, there's an important story that I need you to tell me."

Heath turns and leans against a table. His eyes suddenly have an extra sparkle to them, and I almost forget what I was going to say.

He doesn't speak. Just waits for me to keep talking.

"I need to know—" I say, catching myself before I mix up my words, "—the origin of Diesel's name."

"Really?" A teasing grin crosses his face. "You'd really like to hear that story?"

"Yeah." I quickly reflect on our first phone call and I remember how excited Heath sounded when he tried to tell me the story behind his son's name.

"I have a feeling," I say, "that your Lola hated the notion of Diesel's name at first, and I want to know how you changed her mind."

Heath crosses his arms over his chest, pretending to look smug and superior. "So," he says in a dramatic voice, "Miss Sassy Cassie wants to hear the tale of —"

"Yes, yes, I do." I laugh. "Tell me how it happened."

"Alright. Well, I've always loved the smell of diesel, and Lola hated it. We had an incident once while filling up a van with diesel and it got all over us. I screamed out, 'It's a sign! It's a sign! We name our boy Diesel!' And then Lola started laughing and I was laughing and…" He shrugs. "That's pretty much it."

I giggle at him trying to keep a straight face. "You have a way with cracking people up, Heath. It's a talent."

"Why thank you, Cass," Heath says and pulls out a dorky dance move. He laughs with me as he goes to pay for his comic book. "What do you say to taking a picture with Birdwell?"

"Sure."

We ask Mr. Birdwell to take a picture of us posing with a stack of old encyclopedias, and then we ask his daughter to take a picture of us standing on either side of him and his walker.

We're all smiles.

Eighteen

Heath

When I cook pasta that night, I don't admit to Diesel that it's really just to practice for whenever I get the honor of serving dinner to Cassie. But I should've known how bad it would flop.

"You can't even make spaghetti right, Dad. The noodles are all sticky and smooshed together."

"Pretend it's meant to look like that," I say. "Make me feel better."

Diesel raises his shoulders in a dramatic sigh and takes another bite. "Sauce is alright."

"Yeah. That's because I just heated up what was in a can."

"Dad, if we're gonna have Cassie come over, we have to do our normal and best routine. Order and delivery."

I chuckle as I fork a gloppy ball of pasta and put it into my mouth. "Agreed."

"Ask her soon. She should see our house and then I can see if she she likes me too."

"You're gonna bring out your fart machine, aren't you, Diesel? See if she laughs at it."

"Well, c'mon, Dad, its how we know she's got the same humor as us. We gotta know."

Kid's got a point, I think as I watch him try to hide a fistful of detested spaghetti strands into his napkin.

But I can prod Cassie's sense of humor a little more in my own way too.

Nineteen

Heath

I'm so amused by Cassie making sure there's a gap when we sit at the diner counter. Today she appears more at ease and shares earbuds with me to watch *Smokey And The Bandit* on my laptop—yet every few minutes she glances down to see where our legs are on the stools and scoots half an inch away if she deems it necessary. I keep having to follow her little by little because of her constant movement in order to not lose my earbud.

"What do you think of it so far?" I ask. "Pretty funny, right? You've giggled a few times."

"Yeah," she says, taking another bite of waffle.

"I just love that I get to introduce this movie to you, Cass. It was me and my dad's favorite."

She looks from the laptop screen to her phone, barely responsive to me.

Back to the drawing board, I think. *Old fashioned in-depth conversing.*

"Cass," I say, "were you ever jealous of the class clowns?"

"You mean like did I wish I could be the funny one and never get in trouble for acting stupid?"

"That's one way to put it."

Cassie looks into space and takes a bite of her burnt toast. "Well, I guess I thought it'd be fun to be more of a crazy, window-breaking deviant." She glances at me. "Like you."

"And you didn't want to be known as the funny person? Ever? Because that's what I wanted to be."

"I might've called you funny back then, Heath, if I hadn't been the target of your pranks. It's always funnier when the bad things are happening to someone else."

I lean forward, grabbing my newly refilled cup of coffee. "There wasn't a tiny part of you that thought I was funny when we were teens?"

"Um, no."

"You're lying."

"Am not. I thought you were a jerk." Cassie gives me a half-smile. "A cute jerk, but a jerk."

"I accept that," I say. "We all have glaring flaws that mix with our good qualities. In fact, I can name a glaring flaw of yours right now."

"Which is?" she asks.

"You're very… well… let's just say that one of your best qualities is also your worst. Your stubbornness. I have a love and hate pull toward it."

Cassie bites her lip as she takes the earbud from her ear. She doesn't say a word, but she cough-laughs into her coffee.

Didn't make her mad. Made her laugh again. YES.

Twenty

Heath

Cassie surprises me by coming along for another visit to Mr. Birdwell's garage sale. She said she wanted to see if there was a *Back To The Future* shirt that was in her size and also be on the hunt for any neon-colored travel mugs.

I'm initially feeling compelled to ask her why she is seeking out travel mugs because she doesn't seem like the long distance traveling type, but a better question arises while I watch her dig through several yellow boxes.

"Do you wanna come over tonight and have dinner with me and Diesel?"

Cassie pauses. She doesn't look at me but I can tell she's working on how to best react.

"I'm going to assume," she finally says, "that you've been holding that question back for a long time."

"To be fair," I say, walking around to the other side of the table so that I can see her face, "you technically have already met Diesel. And if it makes you feel better, coming to my house won't count as a date. A date will only be official if done in public."

She shrugs as she returns to sifting through the boxes, creating a symphonic clatter when she knocks a stack of cups over. "That makes some sense."

"You go home as quick as you want after eating dinner with us," I say. "I won't try any funny business."

"Diesel's gonna ask me a million questions, isn't he?"

"Yes."

"You two aren't gonna grade me on wifey or mommy skills, are you?"

I sense a teasing tone in her voice and grin. "Then you're up for it?"

"As long as I can bring my dog. She's accustomed to me being with her at night."

"No problem, Cass. Diesel will give Odessa all the attention she wants."

"Okay." Cassie smiles as she lifts up a neon blue and white travel mug and hugs it like it's a plush toy. "I'll come for dinner, Heath."

I can hardly contain my thrill, and briefly consider trying to do a backflip or a sexy hip hop move.

Cassie Wicker is coming to my house.

***

Cassie's arrival puts Diesel into a mode I've rarely seen from him—he asks her in the most polite manner if he can take her coat and puts said coat on the rack which I didn't even know he knew existed. He doesn't bounce around like I expect him to when Cassie takes off Odessa's leash, but instead asks in a very calm voice, "Is it a girl dog?"

"Yeah." Cassie bends down next to Diesel as they both pet her super cute collie. "Her name's Odessa."

I think it's sweet how welcoming and gentle Diesel is behaving, but I know it won't take long for him to start shooting off at the mouth like usual.

"How old is she?" Diesel blurts. "Does she have any puppies? Did you get her from a shelter? I have three tennis balls in my room that I don't use. She can play with them."

"Sorry, Cass," I say from the kitchen. "He's just really excited to have you over."

"I can tell," Cassie says. She leaves Diesel to play with Odessa and watches me as I go to the fridge. "Do you need me to help with anything, Heath?"

"Just tell me what you'd like to drink. I got water, raspberry iced tea, orange juice, and Dr. Pepper."

"Water is fine."

"Ice?"

"Yeah." She takes the glass that I hand to her. "Thanks."

She sips it while wandering into the living room, once in awhile smiling at Diesel and Odessa's impromptu chasing game.

I busy myself setting the table, starting with opening the eight boxes of Chinese food that I ordered—each one packed with different types of noodles, rice, and veggies—and spooning it into eight separate serving dishes. While I know I may look a bit crazy doing all this extra work, it's part of what keeps me from losing my mind over the clean-up. And I'm quite proud as I go about this routine until I hear Cassie and Diesel loudly talking about me.

"Does your dad always do that?"

"You mean how he's taking every single food out of the containers and putting it into separate bowls?"

Cassie laughs at the way Diesel explains it. "Yes. That."

"He does that a lot. I think it's because he likes to organize stuff like a scientist."

"A scientist," I laugh. I've now moved on to setting out plates and utensils. "More like a con artist trying to pass off someone else's delicious work as my own."

"Dad, you can't cook anything like this."

"I know, Dees. That's why we ordered it. Way to insult me in front of our lovely guest."

"Well, I'm gonna eat it no matter what," Cassie says. "Starving." She grins at me, letting me know that she's on my side.

"Me too," Diesel says. "Can you sit next to me, Cassie?"

"Yes, I will."

"Can I give some of my food to Odessa?"

"Just a few pieces. I brought her kibble along so she can eat her own food with us."

"Oh, that's good," Diesel says. He sits down and smiles when Cassie sits in the chair right beside him. He watches me sit across from Cassie and quickly frowns as his eyes rove the table. "Dad, I think you overdid it."

"What? What'd I overdo?"

Diesel points at the table with a finger, then opens his hand and does a sweeping motion with his whole arm. "Tablecloth. Too much, Dad. Cassie knows guys don't use a tablecloth every night. You're gonna freak her out."

While Cassie seems quite charmed and amused by Diesel's

comments, I'm struck with a tinge of embarrassment.

Tablecloth. Shoot. Your kid's right, Deitrich. You look desperate.

"Cass," I say, meeting her eyes as she puts a forkful of chow mein in her mouth, "be honest. The tablecloth. Is it too much?"

"It's cute, Snakebait," she says.

I smile in relief and then watch Diesel shovel rice into his mouth like he's a champion speed eater.

Forget about reiterating table manners, I think. *Sigh. This kid.*

We enjoy the food, interjecting light commentary here and there about favorite dishes, my subpar cooking skills, and how everyone's day was.

Then Diesel asks in a boisterous tone, "Cassie, why did you start calling my dad 'Snakebait'?"

Twenty-One

Cassie

"Do you wanna tell the story, Heath, or should I?"

"Up to you." Heath chuckles into his glass. "He'll think it's weird either way."

"So," Diesel says, "tell me what happened."

I figure since Diesel is looking right at me that I'll be the one who opens this can of worms. I set my fork down and say, "That nickname came about on the same day your dad started calling me 'Shortbread'. I picked 'Snakebait' because he—"

"I kissed her when I should've given her the Heimlich," Heath says. "She was choking on a shortbread cookie." He gives me a half-smile, silently communicating to me that he's fine being the one to call himself out. "And she said that my breath smelled like fish bait."

"Yeah," I say, "but he already had girls calling him a snake because of how sly and cunning he was."

Diesel has slid down in his chair and has a slight scowl on

his face. "That's not weird," he says to us. "That's dumb."

"Well, you asked, dude," Heath says.

Diesel then looks at me. "Cassie, why'd you make Dad go to juvie?"

"It was just to scare him. Didn't work though."

"But what did he do to go there?"

I look at Heath and watch him sit back in his chair with an expression that says he's eager to hear my version of his 'bad boy' era.

"Well, for one thing," I say to Diesel, "your dad spent an entire afternoon breaking all the windows of the school with bricks. Glass was everywhere. And then he did the same thing to ten other buildings in town."

Diesel has a faint smile as he looks from me to his dad. "And she told on you."

"Yep. But allow me to offer my defense, Cass," Heath says to me, folding his arms on the table. "I did all that because my parents had beat me for two nights straight. I was pissed. Had to let steam out."

"I'm really sorry about that, Heath. Honestly. But I just had to say something or you wouldn't have stopped being a maniac until every business in town was boarded up and made to look like we were bound for a hurricane."

Heath looks at me and then at Diesel. He gives a shrug and puts a big piece of orange chicken into his mouth, chewing it ever so slowly.

The conversation quickly dies—I think that's my fault, and I figure I should just resume eating.

It stays quiet at the table for awhile, but the solemn mood is abruptly broken by a high-pitched, mechanical sounding fart. Diesel immediately giggles, and in a split second the sound comes again.

Oh cheez, I think. *Heath will think I'm way immature if I bust up laughing at a fart.*

I know it's one of those cheap plastic fart machine toys, but I can't help but find it funny—a goofy noise coming out of the blue.

I'm more easily tickled by such things these days... must be an effect that hanging out with Heath has on me.

I don't realize I'm staring into space until I see Heath rolling his eyes and Diesel staring at me.

"I know that was fake," I say.

"Yeah, but you almost laughed, Cassie," Diesel says. "I saw you."

"I do like some juvenile humor, including the bathroom-related type."

"Just not all the time, Diesel," Heath chimes in. "Please, don't put that thing on a loop."

"I won't," Diesel says while looking at me. "I just wanted to know if she thought it was funny."

"I did," I say.

Diesel simply grins and leaves the table. He comes running back with Odessa at his heels. "Cassie," he says while crouching to give her a belly rub, "do you like superheroes?"

I answer him while Heath starts clearing dishes. "Yeah, I do like them, Diesel."

"Who's your favorite?"

"Um, well, I like—"

"Please don't say Wonder Woman!" Diesel yells, dramatically falling to the floor.

Heath looks back from the sink and laughs with me.

"Why's that?" I ask Diesel.

"Well, no offense, but it's because that would just be too predictable for you."

"That's sound logic actually," Heath says. "I have to agree with my precocious son."

He sees me start to get up—assuming I'm going to help with the dishes—and motions for me to stay where I'm at. "No need, Cass. Just relax."

I nod, returning my attention to Diesel. "I really love Batman."

"Just like my dad does."

"Yeah." I would add more to the superhero convo, but once I watch Diesel run off again with Odessa—the two of them sliding around in the hallway like it's a magical ice rink—I know I should at least try to see if Heath will accept any help. Stepping up behind him, I can't believe how fast he is placing the dishes and utensils in the sink.

"You don't have a dishwasher?" I ask.

"I am the dishwasher," Heath says, emphasizing the word 'I'.

For some reason, this is turning out to be the most attractive sight to grace my eyes—a single dad covered in dish soap. I didn't think I had any housewife instincts in me but Heath is making me want to know what it's like to be one.

I hate that I love watching him. I might start drooling like a goopy, heart-eyed fangirl any minute.

Heath is vigorous with his scrubbing. Bubbles fly everywhere each time he unnecessarily squirts more dish soap into the sink.

"You've got an interesting method there."

"You making fun of me?" he asks with a playful smile over his shoulder.

"No," I say. "Just observing. But you're sure I can't help you?"

"No, no. I got this, Cass."

I move off to the side to get a better view of Heath in his cleaning mode. "What do you usually think about when you're doing this?"

"When I'm cleaning?"

"Yeah."

"I sort through the past week's events and have fantasies about the current woman who's in my life."

I expect him to chuckle after he says that, but he doesn't. He's being totally serious. And I'm ninety percent sure I know what woman is on his mind.

"Me," I blurt. "I'm the one you're fantasizing about."

"You are very hard to get out of my head, Shortbread. That's absolutely true. But, just so you know, most of the fantasies I have right now are fairly innocent."

"Really? Innocent?"

"One of them involves you and me and a weekend getaway at a lake house."

I laugh, circling backward. "There is no chance that one stays innocent."

"Okay, maybe not," he says, carrying a stack of plates to the cupboard, "but the current scene in my mind is only up to the part where you ask for a kiss on the dock. And then it's you wrapped in my arms, making out with me like I just returned from six months lost at sea."

"I knew you would go there."

"Go where?" He lowers his voice to a whisper when Diesel walks past us. "Still innocent, Cass. Just kissing."

"Tongue," I whisper back, my cheeks flaring bright red as I can't stop myself from adding to Heath's scenario. "Your tongue would be in my throat. And then I'd be biting your face."

His eyes widen as he backs me into the refrigerator. "Who's

not innocent now, Shortbread?"

I read the mischievousness in his body language—he's unashamedly indulging his own fantasy of chasing and cornering me. "You're still the naughty one, Snakebait," I say.

Heath silently grins as he backs away from me and goes to the counter.

Checking the time on my phone, I start calculating how to avoid staying later than necessary. I can hear Diesel throwing the ball for Odessa in one of the other rooms.

"Are you good for a cup of coffee, Cass?"

"Yeah, I'll have some," I say. "Then I gotta get Odessa to bed."

"Your dog has a bedtime?"

"Sort of."

I'm just making excuses. Feel so conflicted. This is the guy I once wanted to push down an elevator shaft, and now we just had an amazing episode of fiery flirting in his kitchen.

I look over at the couch in the living room as I return to the same chair I had sat in during dinner.

"You drink it black, right?" Heath asks.

It takes me a second to remember that he's making us coffee. I clear my throat before answering. "Yeah, I do."

"You okay?"

"Fine."

When Heath sets a mug before me, I quickly get to drinking it. He laughs while lifting his mug to his mouth. "Wow. Someone's in a rush to bail on me."

I smirk at his teasing and take off my glasses to have something to fidget with. "So, how long have you lived in this house?"

"About seven years."

"Do you like most of your neighbors?"

"Pretty much. We've stayed here as long as we have mostly for Diesel's sake."

"You don't want to take him from his friends?"

"Yeah," Heath says, "but it's also just been the plan. Lola and I agreed to settle in one place for as long as possible once we bought a house. With her gone, I continue things here for Dees."

"That's good." I smile as I sip my coffee. "He's lucky to have you."

"We're both lucky. I didn't know I'd love having a kid this much."

Suddenly feeling a sappy air in the conversation, and not having a clue about how to elaborate or add to the topic of kids, I bite my lip in the struggle to come up with a totally off-the-wall question.

But Diesel runs in, sliding on the floor in his socks, and saves me from being awkward.

"Dad," he says to Heath, "did you buy the hair stuff for my costume?"

"The colored spray, yeah. It's in my bathroom."

"Can I bring it into my room?"

Diesel chuckles into his coffee. "Are you going to try it out in there and make a huge mess?"

"No. I just want to hold onto it."

"I don't trust that smile, dude. Wait for Halloween."

"Aww!" Diesel groans and looks at me. "Cassie, my dad's got too many rules."

"No, I don't." Heath says shortly.

I giggle at his peeved tone and try to distract Diesel for him. "What's your costume?"

"Tony Stark," Diesel says proudly. "Dad's gonna make my hair dark brown. And I've got a professional business suit and everything."

"You're gonna be Tony Stark and not Iron Man?"

"I was Iron Man last year. Gotta be a different costume."

"I get that," I say.

"What are you gonna be, Cassie?"

"I don't know yet."

"So, I know you don't have kids," Diesel says to me, "but do you dress up and take Odessa for a walk on Halloween?"

"I do dress up, but I just stay home and pass out candy."

Diesel bounces the tennis ball several times, looking hard at me and then at Heath. It seems like they're reading each other's minds because as soon as Diesel gives a silly, slow motion pointing gesture to himself, then to me, and then to Heath, Heath clears his throat and says, "Cass, would you like to walk around on Halloween with me and Diesel this year?"

"I guess I could," I say. "I always love watching families have fun out there."

"And you'll bring your dog?" Diesel asks.

"No." I get up to put my coffee mug in the sink. "Odessa gets overstimulated around lots of kids. But I'll go with you guys."

"Yay!"

Diesel busts out a smooth dance move and motions for me to high-five him. Once I oblige, he zooms back to his room.

Heath laughs, shaking his head, and leans against the refrigerator. A few poufy bits of hair fall in his eyes.

"When it's you hanging out with me AND Diesel, Cass, we can just call it a family outing. Unless… that makes you more uncomfortable than calling it a date."

"Casual group outing," I say. "Let me know what time you're

going trick-or-treating with Diesel and I'll be here."

"Absolutely will."

I pace near the door, silently wishing Heath would give me a legitimate reason to leave, but he just stands there smiling at me.

"What's your costume, Heath?" I ask. "Or do you not dress up?"

"Oh, I always dress up. But you don't have any idea of what you wanna be?"

"Well, actually," I say, "I just got an idea. Like, really, just this second."

"Oh yeah? Tell me."

"No way. I don't want you to end up matching me."

"Ah, so it must be a couple costume."

I shake my head as Heath walks toward me. "It's not."

"Then I'm not saying mine either, Cass. You'll just see for yourself."

Great, I think. *I wonder what wild, fantastical creature Heath will be.*

Twenty-Two

Heath

I never have a problem deciding on a Halloween costume. Usually I dress up as a character from a movie that I recently watched, and this year that character is Andrew Clark from *The Breakfast Club*.

I could've been jock material in high school, I think, if only I had channeled my rock-throwing skill into swinging a bat.

I put on my thrifted varsity jacket and look behind me as Diesel runs into my room.

"Dad, what do you think Cassie's costume is?"

"I have no idea," I say.

"Didn't she tell you she liked Batman? Maybe she'll be Batgirl."

"Highly doubt that."

"Then she might be Catwoman or just a cat. Or maybe she'll be a nurse or flight attendant, or maybe—"

"Dees," I say, cutting into his hyper run-on sentence, "look in the mirror. Do you like how your hair came out?"

"Yeah. It's really cool. But we need to go now, Dad. Ryan and Isaac and all the guys are gonna beat me to the best houses."

"Okay, okay, dude. We're going."

I walk outside with him and turn to lock the door. When I turn back around, I see Cassie.

And Cassie is dressed as—wouldn't you know it—the emo basket case Allison from *The Breakfast Club.*

"I think my heart just stopped," I say, dramatically pressing a hand to my chest.

"Why?" Cassie looks so oblivious as she sifts through her purse.

"You are my girl."

"I'm what?"

"Cass, look at me." I spread my arms. "I'm the jock from that movie. Andrew Clark."

Cassie lifts her head, shaking her bangs out of her eyes. She seems bewildered as she looks at me and then looks down at herself. Looks at me again. And then it finally registers in her brain.

"Oh, shiiii—" she exclaims, stopping just short of cussing in front of Diesel—which honestly, I would have found even funnier.

"Oh yes," I say with a laugh.

"This is not a couple costume," Cassie says, "and you know it."

"By the end of the movie they sure are a couple, Shortbread. And YOU know it."

She rolls her eyes at the way I mimicked her irritated voice. "Dang it, Heath! How did this happen? You didn't sneak into my house earlier, did you?"

"I did not. I promise you." I give a quick nod to Diesel when he motions that he's going to follow his friends. "We're just two great minds thinking alike."

"You and I," Cassie says, waving a finger in the air, "need to keep a four foot distance between us when we walk."

"Why?"

"This could end up being so humiliating, and we have to have a buffer zone. I don't like the idea of anyone I know out here to catch me in this ill-timed accident."

"You don't have to be so shy, Cass. It's not the end of the world."

"I'm not shy. I just don't want to be part of a couple costume."

"Well, it looks like fate intervened."

Cassie shakes her head as we walk along. "Fate. Stupid fate."

Wonderful fate, I think.

I throw Cassie's suggestion of a "four foot distance" out the window and bump my shoulder into hers. She doesn't look at me, but she doesn't sprint away either. I lower my hand until I feel her palm brush against mine.

Twenty-Three

Cassie

Heath touches the tips of my fingers with his and cracks up when I react by punching his arm.

"Cheez, girl!" he teases. "You act like I've got cooties."

"If you had cooties, Snakebait, I would've punched you in a different place."

"Rawr." Heath's deep, drawn out chuckle follows me as I walk ahead. "Little tigress comin' to the surface."

"You keep it quiet with the flirting." I turn, pressing my fist into his shoulder. "I swear if someone I know hears you saying that to me—"

"Cassie?"

Uh oh. A shrill voice I would recognize anywhere. Another former classmate—a former cheerleader.

"Crud," I groan. "Heath, walk away before she—"

"Cassie, it's me! Jill!"

I cringe as Jill steps in my path. She was the cheerleader who had four boyfriends in five months. She apparently now has a husband and four kids with her.

"We just moved into the neighborhood last week," she says in an overly bright tone.

"Hi, Jill." I fix a button on my jacket as I cope with Jill and her family unapologetically staring at me and Heath.

"You remember me, right, Cassie? I was at your school for my junior year. We had a couple classes together."

"Yes," I say with a forced smile. "We sure did."

"And aren't you Heath Deitrich?" Jill zeroes in on Heath as he unwraps a piece of gum and puts it in his mouth. "Weren't you two sworn rivals?"

"Absolutely," Heath says with a wink in my direction. "But we've cleared things up now."

Oh no, I think. *Heath, you aren't helping the situation!*

"You guys got married?" Jill asks. She sounds exuberant as if she has just heard the best gossip of the year.

"No," I say with a huff. "Both single. He is a single dad. I'm a single dog mom. I'm just walking along with him and his kid."

"Well…" She looks us up and down, tilting her head as her husband puts his arm around her. "I love the costumes."

"Thanks." I have no emotion on my face or in my voice. Dry as I can be. "Was not planned."

And then Jill trades a smirk with her husband before the two of them move on to catch up to their kids. I know what they are thinking and I wish I had some Gatorade to dump on their heads. "See you around!" she calls back to me.

I look at Heath and see his mischievous smile.

"Yeah. Real great," I say.

"What's the big deal? We look like we could be together, Cass."

"I'm so glad I did not let you hold my hand."

"Yes, but that would've been brilliant." Heath keeps pace with me as we look ahead to see where Diesel went. "I would've sold the couple performance if you had let me."

"I don't want rumors to get out. It'll be like high school all over again."

"Then why are you looking at me as if I was the last piece of dark chocolate in a wrapper?"

"I'm not. And you couldn't sound any weirder, Heath."

"Yes I can. I can yell out our nicknames to the neighborhood in a high-pitched Irish accent."

"Don't you dare," I say.

"Watch me." He slowly starts backing away while counting. "1… 2…"

"Heath, don't."

But the second that he yells it out, I just start laughing and he breaks into laughter with me.

"I know, I know," he says. "Worst accent ever, right?"

"A little," I say. "But still funny."

Heath spots Diesel and calls for him to come back toward us. As we wait for Diesel to finish whatever silly conversation he is having with his friends in the road, I find myself overflowing with admiration for Heath and his role as a dad.

"How many more years you think you got left before Diesel thinks you're not cool to trick or treat with?"

"Good question, Cass. Unfortunately, I'm thinking this might be the last one. You see how he has no problem leaving us in the dust."

"Yeah. But you seem like you've been a really fun dad. I don't know if he will be quick to completely ditch you."

Heath quietly smiles at me right before Diesel pops up

between us like an elated kangaroo. Several pieces of candy spill in the process.

"Hey, Dad! Dad!"

"What's up, my dude?" Heath asks. "You lost some of your hard-earned treasure there."

"But I have to ask you something, Dad. It's important."

"Okay. Ask me."

"Can we go to the zoo this weekend?"

"Um…" Heath shoots me an expression that says he is just about had it with his kid's questions. He sighs, looks at Diesel who has his arms crossed, and says, "Where on Earth did that come from? I haven't heard you talk about the zoo in months."

"I'm doing a report on giraffes. I need to see them up close."

Heath glances at me, sees my amused smile, and chuckles as he turns back to Diesel. "Is this your way of getting me, you, and Cassie on another group excursion?"

"Only if you see it that way, Dad," Diesel says in a very matter-of-fact way. His whole demeanor right now matches his slick Tony Stark costume. "Cassie, you really should come with us because my dad will get you a pretzel."

Noticing Diesel's wink at me, I decide to play along with his low-key coercing. "Yes, Heath, I'll follow you guys there, but only if you buy me and Diesel soft pretzels and lemonade."

"I've gotta spoil both of you?" Heath asks with a smile.

"Yup. Cassie and I have to get the best snacks."

Heath rolls his eyes. He looks at me and says, "Just for a couple hours, Cass? You don't have to stay for very long."

"Sounds fun."

I'm enjoying his company, I really am, I think, *but do I want to be a couple? Not worth the complications. It was never worth it with anyone else I've dated.*

But this is Heath Alun Deitrich we're talking about! And he is the one I never in a million years wanted to be with... yet, he's proving to be different. Different than every other man I know.

"Hey, Shortbread, before you go," Heath says, "we need a picture."

"Fair enough, Snakebait."

I turn, tilting my head with a silly grin next to him as he looks at me with an extra serious face. "What's the grumpy look for?" I ask before he taps the button on his phone. "Want me to look like that too?"

"Whatever you want. It's just us being goofy."

"Okay." I change my expression to an overly posed shocked face while Heath keeps to his serious one.

* * *

Heath texts the picture to me two hours later when I'm half-asleep on the couch with Odessa and snuggled under a pile of eight blankets.

The image of us in our matching costumes gives me butter-flies.

We totally look like a couple, I think. *Unplanned. Annoying.*

But it's sort of cool...

Twenty-Four

Cassie

It's a nice breezy day for the zoo, I think, watching Diesel dash ahead of us. *Sun is out. Lovely mild weather. But I have doubts about why we all came out here... I'm sure Diesel has a reasoning other than doing research for a school project.*

"Heath," I say, "does your kid really have to write a report on giraffes?"

"I honestly half-believed him until you just said that."

We laugh and Heath points to one of the snack carts. "Want something?"

"A soda would be nice. Sprite."

"Done. Be back in a few."

I smile after him and then look to see where Diesel went. The kid moves fast.

"Cassie!" Diesel springs out from behind a cluster of bushes and wildly waves at me to follow him. "C'mere! You gotta see this."

"What?"

"Just c'mere."

I'm halfway to running when Diesel skids to a halt in front of the tiger exhibit. "Look, Cassie, they're fighting each other like you and my dad used to do."

"I think they're just playing. Play-fighting."

"Well, they sort of remind me of you and my dad."

"Heath and I were nothing like tigers," I say with a chuckle. "Let's go look at the reptiles and I'll point out which is most like Heath in there."

"Why?" Diesel walks backward with a sly grin. "Because he's YOUR 'Snakebait'?"

Oh gosh, I think. *I must be blushing now.*

"Very funny," I say without a smile.

"I'm being serious," Diesel says as he turns around. "You and my dad are epic together."

Just as I'm thinking of a well-worded response to that, I hear Heath coming up behind me.

"Hey, Cass, is Diesel talking your ear off over here?"

I look at Heath's face, then down at the soda bottle in his hand. "Yeah. I just thought we should go check out the reptiles."

"For sure. Here's your soda."

"Thanks." I take it as carefully as I can from him, avoiding any contact between our fingers. And Heath notices—smiles and shakes his head at my timid maneuver. "Cass, you're silly."

"Yeah, I try."

"Wanna try out a few different picture-taking locations?" He points behind me. "I'm thinking that we either include the flamingos in our selfie or the monkeys."

"Flamingos," I say. "Their colors are gorgeous and I feel tranquil near them."

Heath looks like he's about to debate me on it, but shrugs with a grin and heads to the right. He waves for me to follow him. "Flamingos it is, Cassie. Diesel can catch up."

I make sure that Diesel did, in fact, hear what his dad said and give him a smile before walking after Heath.

Heath chooses to pose by the flamingo exhibit with a cocky, smoldering look. I end up standing with my back to his, rolling my eyes at him just as he takes the picture.

We both giggle like little kids when he texts it to me right then and there and we see how we look.

"Now, THAT is a memory for all time," Heath says as he gleefully admires the picture on his phone.

He is so full of life, I think. *I should feel outright lucky to be standing next to him.*

The day turns out to be one of the most relaxing I've had in awhile, and what makes me laugh even more on my drive back home is realizing that we never once looked at the giraffes.

Diesel. What a sly little dude.

Twenty-Five

Heath

We spend our next few breakfast dates watching movies on my laptop. Cassie still only wants to sit at the counter instead of in a booth, and while it's not as comfortable, I have to admit that I like her stubborn energy.

She's an absolute adventure of her own make, I think. *A sweet and endearing adventure.*

"What are you doing for Thanksgiving?" I ask during the last half hour of *Rudy*.

"Not much," Cassie says. "I don't like big gatherings or making a fuss over an extravagant holiday meal."

"You can have Thanksgiving with me and Diesel. We'll just pick up something simple."

"Thanks, but I'm taking that day to lay low with Odessa and my TV reruns."

"Well," I say, forking a piece of sausage, "that honestly sounds nice too."

"But you can ask me to come over for Christmas."

"Oh?" I look at Cassie, seeing her pretend that she's not tearing up at the movie. "You'd really spend Christmas with me?"

"Christmas Eve," she says. "I'll be glad to make and bring dessert for you guys."

"That would be amazing, Cass."

She silently smiles and tilts her head.

"And, you know," I say, leaning back in my chair, "I'm just wondering, is there any chance I ever get to come see your house?"

"It's very messy, Heath. It'll take me forever to organize all the photos I just printed."

"I can help you with that."

"With what?"

"Your photos. We can categorize them and stick them in the albums according to the date and specific adventure."

"You just want to see more of my private world, don't you?"

"I do," I say. "Not gonna lie."

Cassie doesn't verbalize her agreement, but she smiles into her coffee.

I smile back, then take a neon green squirt gun out of my coat pocket, place it on the counter, and slide it over to her.

Twenty-Six

Cassie

Heath has just gifted me a squirt gun—a squirt gun that's actually filled with water—and a sticky note taped to it with a message written in Sharpie: **Have Your Revenge, Sassy Cassie.**

A clear and brazen nod to the way in which he used to piss me off—the squirt gun incident that occurred every single week in our high school assembly.

One of the many incidents we had recently been reminiscing on, and he has it in him to allow me a measure of payback?

Heath winks when I look at him.

I pick up the neon squirt gun, enjoying the power I'm suddenly feeling, and by the time I've gathered my purse and stood up, I see Heath running as fast as he can out the diner with his own squirt gun in hand.

I forget that I'm an adult. I bolt after him, childish giggles overtaking me.

This is war.

We go at each other with our squirt guns—very quick, albeit pathetic bursts—pretending that the diner parking lot and all the cars in it are fantastic hiding places to spring on each other from.

The game is short and sweet and very satisfying.

Within six minutes, Heath pretends his squirt gun has malfunctioned.

"Finish the job, girl!" he shouts. "Make me your prisoner."

Then he pretends to pass out on the hood of his car.

"Ha, ha. Convincing, Heath." I fling my now-empty squirt gun at him. "You can keep this. I'll count the duel as a mental souvenir for our date."

Heath rights himself and gets into his car as I get into mine. "Happy to help," he says. "When am I coming over? You pick the day."

"The day before Christmas Eve. Does that work?"

"Definitely does."

"And you like brownies, right?"

"Oh, you know I would never turn down one of your sweet treats."

"Glad to know," I say. "I'll have some for us to snack on."

Heath leans out his window, watching as I back out of the parking space. "Hey, Shortbread," he says, grinning wide when I look at him, "I'm excited to spend Christmas with you."

I nervously smile back, anxiety flooding my chest.

This sure will be a core memory, I think. *I've not had a guy come into my house for a long, long time.*

Stopping at a light, I drum on my steering wheel, working out in my head about how I'll explain the clutter in my house and the rows of bright cereal boxes on my kitchen counter that a woman my age shouldn't have stockpiled.

Maybe Heath won't notice any of those things. Maybe he won't want to snoop around the way I do at someone's house.

Then again, his consistent curiosity and fascination of me will probably get the better of him.

I just gotta accept that I may be judged for my home and all that is a part of it—but I'll be spending time with the sweetest, funniest man in the world.

That fact alone should lift my spirits high.

Twenty-Seven

Heath

The first thing I notice in Cassie's house is the aroma of fresh brownies overlaid with citrus. I really didn't know what I expected of her place, but the beautiful open floor plan and polished staircase is quite a contradiction to the precarious stacks of ragged boxes that take up every corner.

"You look like you're in the midst of moving somewhere, Cass."

"I'm not," she says as she plates the brownies. "It's just my slapdash method of rearranging things."

"You have a very big house."

"Yeah, and?"

"Nothing. Just curious how you've got to this point in life."

"Maybe because I'm good with finances." She puts a brownie on a napkin and hands it to me. "And I've had crazy success not just with catering desserts but my sticker business too. Feels more like luck than anything."

"Hard work," I acknowledge. "I can see that. Plus, I'm thinking that Odessa likes the extra room to run around in here."

Cassie smiles, watching me kneel down and tousle Odessa's ears. "Yeah," she says. "It's her castle too for sure."

I look around at the bare walls, noting that there isn't any decor hung up anywhere.

"You don't frame pictures?"

"I'm not big on putting anything up on my walls or framing things. I'd just knock into them in my clumsy moments."

"Not even movie posters? I'd assume you have an entire stockpile of those."

"I have some posters, just put away in a box upstairs."

I watch Cassie go into her kitchen and follow, glancing at the photos laid out on a long table. "This where we're gonna organize your photos?"

"Yeah. Lining them up with labels."

"And what's all this stuff?" I sit down and start flipping through a notebook.

"Journals and notebooks from school. I've been going through them just for fun." Cassie brings the plate of brownies to the table and then looks at me with an empty mug in hand. "Want coffee?"

"I'd love some," I say.

She smiles and goes to work grinding beans. I just enjoy the view of her standing in her kitchen.

"Cass, where are your yearbooks?"

"I burned them."

"You what?"

"Burned them. Some time ago."

"Huh," I say, looking through one of her journals, "that has to be regretful."

"No. It was cathartic, Heath. I hated those years."

"Well, I saved all of my yearbooks."

Cassie laughs while she brings the coffee to the table. She gives a full mug to me and sits on the opposite side. "I didn't know men could be that sentimental."

"Oh, I am," I say.

While looking through the journal, I suddenly hear Twenty One Pilot's "Stressed Out" playing and glance up to see where it's coming from. Cassie has her tablet beside her and is scrolling through music.

"Keep it on this one," I say. "This is a fave song of mine."

She grins and leaves it on the song, silently watching me dance in my chair and mouth the lyrics.

I move on to start putting Cassie's photos in one of many albums, and I find myself glued to her skydiving photos.

"Wow," I say. "Not one of these shows a guy with you, except for the tandem instructors—which I'll assume were never your dates."

"Yeah. I never dated any fellow adrenaline junkies."

"You love falling," I say, "but not falling in love."

"That's one way to put it."

I clear my throat and scoot my chair back as I hold up a handful of photos, looking like I'm about to dole out playing cards. "And when I look at these photos of you ascending these snowy mountains, Cass, I think to myself, 'My goodness. Now THAT is a keeper. Strong, sexy, fearless. What guy wouldn't want a woman like that in his world'?"

Cassie half-smiles at my poetic gushing, but doesn't respond.

I'm assuming she wants me to drop the subject since she clearly has a rough dating history.

Women are good at ignoring, I think. And good at creating distractions.

So I drop it and begin lining up photos of what looks to be some of her kayaking adventures, and then look at Cassie as she thumbs through a pink journal. She suddenly stops on a random page and stares at it for a long time.

"What is it? Did you write something embarrassing?" I ask. "Funny? Something about me?"

"Evidence of your pranks, Heath," she says.

"Evidence?" I set my mug down. "Let me see."

Cassie hesitates before sliding her hand along the page and picking at a corner.

It's a photo, I realize as she holds it up. *A photo stuck between the pages. And I recognize it.*

"This is so stupid," Cassie says as she looks at it. She bursts into giggles. "I'm not surprised that you did something like this though, Heath. Up your alley of trouble."

I swipe the photo to have a closer look. The image is a close-up of a brick wall with the words '**Snakebait Loves Shortbread**' spray-painted on it.

"That was not a prank, Cass. I meant it in a very serious way."

"I don't remember who took the photo but I know people talked about you spending almost two hours using up an insane amount of spray paint to write this. And I heard that it was supposed to embarrass me since I didn't want anything to do with you."

"I have that same photo," I say. "It's in an envelope on my bookshelf. I'll show you tomorrow night when you come over."

"And why would me seeing you with your own copy of this photo make me believe you were sincere when you wrote that?"

"Because, Cassie," I say fervently, "I glued a tiny picture of seventeen-year-old you to the back of it. And I drew hearts around your name with a Sharpie. I dated it and everything."

"I'm sure you did," Cassie mutters. She picks up her mug and gestures to mine. "Want a refill?"

"I'm good, thanks."

She nods and goes to the coffee pot to get more for herself.

I hold onto the photo, smirking as I know Cassie is trying her best to ditch the conversation surrounding it.

"I should've asked this earlier," Cassie says as she sits back down, "but what's Diesel's favorite dessert? I need to know for tomorrow."

"Caramel cupcakes with cream cheese frosting."

"And do you like that too?"

"Absolutely, Cass. I'm easy to please."

She smiles, tucking a strand of hair behind her ear. "Will do then."

"And I'll be getting us pizza for dinner," I say, "since I can't make anything luxurious."

"That sounds good to me." She glances at her tablet, and then looks at her phone.

"I really should let you go for the night," she says to me. "It's almost ten."

"Not like I have anywhere to be, Cass, but I'll agree with you. As a gentleman." I stand up and give an elegant bow as if she was a queen to say goodnight to.

"Hey, Heath?"

"Yeah?" I ask, pulling my coat on at the door.

Cassie leans against the wall and extends a card out to me. It's a very red, Christmasy card with reindeer all over the front of it.

"Can you give this to Diesel?" she asks. "It's a Christmas

present for him. Him and you."

I look at her, not sure if I'm supposed to open it now, but I see her motion for me to do so. I almost let out an audible "aww" when I see what's inside the card—tickets to the aquarium.

"Cassie, this is so sweet of you."

"Well, I saw how much Diesel loved the zoo so I figure he would appreciate going to the aquarium. More fun animals there."

"Can my present to you be the true story of the writing in this photo?" I ask.

She lets out a soft chuckle. "If it's really true, yes, I'll take that as a perfect gift."

"Good. Then I'll see you tomorrow."

"Yeah."

I walk backward out the door, almost blowing her a kiss, but stop myself just short of doing that.

Don't ruin this civil moment, I tell myself. *Don't mess it up.*

Twenty-Eight

Cassie

The Christmas Eve pizza dinner with Heath and Diesel turns out to be pleasantly uneventful. Diesel opens a few gifts and also gives me a very smiley thank you for the aquarium tickets—I'm betting his dad nudged him into displaying extra enthusiasm. It's eight-thirty by the time we munch through half the tray of my cupcakes, and Diesel has gone on to play with Odessa in another other part of the house.

"Cassie, c'mere." Heath motions for me to join him at his bookshelf. "I gotta show you."

There's no way he has it, I tell myself. *The same decades old photo of the flamboyantly spray-painted words '**Snakebait Loves Shortbread**'? I don't believe it.*

Sensing my impatience, Heath chuckles as he takes an envelope from the very top shelf. He slides a single photo out of it and then sits down on the floor—a risky move at our age because of the hassle to get back up. I sit across from him, tucking one leg beneath me, but then decide to hug my knees to my chest in a sort of infantile security measure. *I'm jittery. Feeling intense butterflies.*

"See?" he says, holding the photo up.

"Wow." I draw in a breath, hesitating to take it and feel its realness, but I let Heath place the photo in my hand.

I look at every detail—the same texture on the wall, same shape and color of the letters, same location—all of it the exact same as is in the photo that I have at home. The one that I had shown Heath.

"It is the same," I say.

"Yeah. And look, turn it over. Look at the back."

I flip it over and explode in a snort-laugh. "Oh my gosh, Heath. You really did glue my yearbook picture on the back of it!"

"Yeah. The hearts drawn on it like I told you."

I want to keep laughing as I look at the picture of myself, but I notice Heath has gotten very serious, and I mirror his expression as I give it back to him.

"This right here," Heath says, gently waving the photo above his head, "is one of my top three proudest moments in all of high school, Shortbread."

"Really?"

"Yes. I spent a good few hours planning the color scheme and shape of each letter before I set out to paint it up on that wall. That was our senior year and we were two months from graduation. I had to declare that message somewhere on campus before you were gone for good."

"But you were still a jerk to me even toward the end."

"I didn't mean for the last two pranks to happen to you. It

was Ian and Todd. I told them I was done partaking in stupid schemes but they did them anyway and I agreed to be the co-conspirator."

"You're crazy," I say, shaking my head. But hearing his explanation makes me smile. "Why didn't you just straight up tell me you liked me?"

"Because you would not have taken me seriously, and because I liked being the complex mystery creature for once instead of that role always played by the girl."

"I'm a complex mystery creature?" I say, adding a dramatic pause between each word.

Heath tilts his head and smiles. "There's a hint of disgust forming in your eyes, Shortbread." He reaches out and boops me on the nose. "That is why I never said I liked you to your face. You would've gone full femme fatale on me."

Femme fatale, I think. *What a colorful, never-before-heard description about me from a cute man's mouth.*

"I don't know if I would've gotten THAT angry," I say.

"Oh, you would've given me a serious ass-kicking, I'm sure."

Our rising banter makes me blush apple red, and I distract myself by pulling out a random yearbook from Heath's book-shelf.

"Heath," I say, keeping my head down as I leaf through pages, "whether or not you had a part in it, that very last prank had me combing sand and toothpaste out of my hair for two days." I laugh to myself. "But it wasn't as horrible as some of your other pranks had been."

Heath stays quiet. I glance at him, feeling jumpy when he reaches out and touches my wrist. He still doesn't say anything, just gently wraps his fingers higher up my arm.

I look back at the yearbook and whisper, "You were really in love with me?"

"Still am. You're a trooper, Cassie Wicker."

I snap my head up, a chill diving down my spine.

The manly purr and seriousness in his voice when he said that. Omg.

"Cass?"

"Yeah?"

"Can I… can I put my arm around you?"

I barely hear my own voice as I respond. "Yes."

Heath scoots to sit right beside me, our backs against the bookshelf. He slowly puts his arm around me, and we look at each other, my stomach feeling like it's being tumble-dried in outer space.

"Are you comfortable?" he asks.

"Yeah, but it's gonna be a pain in the butt to stand up."

"I know," he says with a chuckle. "We're old."

I smile, wondering if I should risk l putting my head on his shoulder.

"This isn't so bad feeling you touch me, Heath. I could get used to it if I had to."

"Oh yeah?" The volume of his voice suddenly crescendos and he shouts with the vigor of a kid about to smoke someone in a game of dodgeball, "What about this?"

He ferociously starts tickling me, grabbing me around the waist as I break into giggly shrieks. I try to push him away but he follows me. We are both in a mess of laughter.

"Snakebait! Snakebait, stop!"

"Want me to stop, Shortbread? Really? 'Cause you're giggling pretty hard and I think you love a good tickle fight."

"Heath!" I laugh. "Heath, quit it! Let me up!"

Heath pins me to the floor, holding my wrists down while he

has a goofy grin on his face. He's clearly enjoying having the high ground as I weakly push back against him.

"I think she loves tickle fights!" Diesel randomly yells from his room.

Heath and I bust up again in tearful laughter. He tries to pull me up but I can't get my balance at all and we collapse together on the floor—Heath lying directly on top of me.

"Wow, Cass," he says between laughs, "it really IS hard to get up off the floor at this age."

I grin, silently thankful when he switches to lying beside me on his back.

We look at the ceiling for a minute and I think back to when I used to lie down in the grass during PE to calm myself after a nerve-shattering game of softball.

I prop myself up with my elbow, finding it more comfortable to lie on my side, and Heath does the same. I can tell that he's gotten himself into a "Romeo-esque" state of mind because he places himself as close as he can to me without our bodies touching, and looks me up and down with boyishly sly eyes.

I try to think of somewhere else to look as his eyes bore through me, but I can only stare back, barely able to breathe, barely able to think.

Heath gingerly runs his fingers up my neck and into my hair, pulling me in so that my forehead is almost pressed to his. He half-smiles, leans to the right of me, and gently breathes on my ear, his hand still on the back of my neck.

Every part of me is trembling. I don't know how to react.

Heath's lips brush along the edge of my ear, making me feel like he could give me a love bite at any second. Then he rests his face against mine, nuzzles his nose against my cheek, and moans just ever so slightly.

And then… his mouth is one inch away from touching mine. *Heath Alun Deitrich is about to kiss me.*

My mind erupts with every doubt, fear, and inconsistent monologue.

Wait! We're kissing?! Right now? I didn't expect this. I do want him to—no. No, I can't. A kiss will lead to a make out session which will lead to an exclusive serious relationship and what if it doesn't work? What if I'm leading him on or he's just using me? Do I let this fantasy play out?

"Cass," Heath whispers, sounding like he's doing his absolute darndest to restrain himself, "can I kiss you?"

I loudly exhale, shaking my head as I scoot away from him. "Sorry. I'm not… I'm so sorry. I'm just not really—"

"It's okay."

"Heath, I swear I'm…I know I'm acting so weird and up and down…"

"It's okay, Cass," he says again. "I'm sorry if I made you uncomfortable. It's just… you're just… incredible."

The playful, adoring desire in his blue eyes sends my stomach into multiple backflips. *I'm scared by how much I like him. If I don't leave his house right now I'll do something totally stupid.*

"Heath," I say in a shaky voice, "can we pick this up tomorrow or next week? I forgot that I have to make a batch of red velvet cupcakes for a client. Need to get a head start on it because it's a huge amount."

Heath's eyes follow me as I pull on my boots. A sweet, mischievous smile very slowly forms on his face when he realizes I'm awkwardly but politely trying to extricate myself from the situation. His silence while we look at each other turns my legs into jello and I stumble forward, catching myself on a chair.

"It's a huge, huge order of cupcakes," I reiterate. "Seventy of them."

"Really? Wow. Then you better get on it, Cass."

Heath's teasing tone gives me chills and I look at him as he opens the front door for me. "Thanks for the info about that photo. Gave some clarity."

"More than clarity," he says. "Now I know for sure that our feelings are on the same wavelength."

He sees right through me. I feel every emotion at once and it's making me dizzy.

"Thanks for the pizza, Heath. It was great." I hope to leave without doing something majorly embarrassing in front of him but almost face-plant on the street. Heath sees my clumsy moment and gently grasps my arm as I reach my car door.

"Shortbread," he says, "you don't have to feel weird about not wanting to kiss me. It's a wild concept, I know."

"Do you have to wink when you say that?"

"Yes." Heath smooths his hair in a dramatic fashion. "It's part of my charm."

"Boyish charm, yeah. You and Diesel got that going for you. I hope you guys enjoy the aquarium."

"We will."

"Good."

"But, you know," he says, "it'd make your present even better if you came with us."

I smile at him, a debate revving up in my head about why I shouldn't go, but I know I should just say yes.

"Absolutely," I say. "That'd be fun, Heath."

I like this man so much it hurts. And he even seems to relish my awkward exits.

Heath gives a wave as I get into my car, and I wave back,

feeling wholly inept, flustered, and like a big bumbling disaster.

Twenty-Nine

Heath

I can't stop thinking about Cassie and I's almost-kiss. I've come close to walking into two different walls in the aquarium since my brain is high on Cassie's scent and the memory of her soft skin. The experience of lying next to her, having her face so close to mine… it was better than perfect.

"Dad, look! The penguin's doing a somersault!"

Diesel's voice brings me back to the present, and I follow him, watching Cassie smiling and making a funny comment about the penguins too.

Two days after Christmas Eve, Diesel informally agreed with me that Cassie completes our family and that he would love if she spent every single day with us. And now, as I see them sharing giggles over animals in the aquarium, I feel nothing but joy. I can totally picture us as a family.

It's now or never.

"Hey, can I talk to you a minute, Cass? Alone?"

She trades shrugs with Diesel and smiles at me. "Sure."

I motion for Diesel to wander around on his own for a bit while Cassie and I walk further past the windows of the penguin exhibit.

"Cass, I know this might come across as maybe forward-sounding or a little out there, but—"

"What is it? You aren't gonna try a fake proposal, are you?"

"No." I look past her at Diesel who is raising his hand for an air-five. I ignore him as I clear my throat. "Thing is, Cass, we know that we really like each other. And Diesel's been talking a lot about us too and where our future could go."

"I'm sure he has."

"Yeah. Well, I just wanted to tell you something that I thought was very sweet... something he said about you."

"What'd he say?"

I hold my breath for a second and cross my arms in my nervousness, wondering about the reaction that I'll get for saying this...

"Heath, what did Diesel say about me? I'm sure I'll be flattered."

"He told me that he would love it if you were his mom." I falter when I see her smile fade. "Said he... wishes... you and I would be together... as a family. Live in our house."

Cassie stares at me, frozen like a DVD put on pause. She doesn't blink. Isn't breathing.

Crap, I think. *I broke her.*

Thirty

Cassie

I feel like I've just swallowed a slab of concrete.

Me? As Diesel's mom? Living with them in their house? Not my house or my alone time? Yes, it's beyond flattering... hearing this is great... and terrifying... I'm almost about to vomit from the sudden stress.

"Cass?"

Why am I stressing? It's all in my head. It's all imaginary. I want Heath in my life... I want him.... but... being a mom? Being Heath's girlfriend and a mom to his kid all at once? What if...?

"Cassie, you okay?"

I need to be sure I'm okay with having a man and his son in my space for the rest of my life.

"Cass?"

"Yeah?"

"What's wrong? You're blanking out on me."

"Sorry. Sorry, it's just that…"

"I know. Never mind what I said. I didn't mean to get so intense with that. It's just, you know, I thought it was cute what Diesel said, and he likes you so much."

"Yeah," I whisper. "A little bit much to take in."

"We're taking things slow, Cassie. There's no pressure for you to be a mom."

"It's not just that, Heath. I have to be sure I'm truly ready and am the best thing for you and Diesel."

"But you are the best. I see how happy you are and have been with me."

He touches his fingers to mine like he did on Halloween, obviously wanting us to hold hands.

I let him.

We stop in front of the effervescent jellyfish exhibit and he smiles. "It can only get better from here, Cass."

I look at the glass, feeling Heath lift my right hand and press it against his chest. I cringe as my stomach flips.

"I need space," I blurt out. "Isolation. My alone time. Like how I did things before you came around."

"Oh, I get it," he says playfully, "the kid thing petrifies you, huh?"

"Well, actually—"

"I promise I'm not gonna rush any parenting business involving you. We're just gonna keep hanging out like we've been doing"

"No, Heath. I mean I need to be alone."

Half of me feels like an idiot expressing it in this manner, but no other words come to mind. It's embarrassing to admit fear to anyone, but telling the truth so bluntly to Heath on a day when we are supposed to just be having fun… it sucks.

I know I'm sounding erratic. I just know it. But I'm scared. So freaking scared.

"Away from you," I say. "No contact at all."

"Why?" He lets go of my hands and touches my cheek. "We're good, Cass."

I lightly push him away, looking into his eyes. I let out a shaky breath. "At least until the wedding rehearsal. We can discuss more about what we both want then."

"I think you know what I want. You know exactly the future I want with you."

"I still have to work through the mental puzzles. My nerves about a future with a maybe husband and—"

"It's no puzzle to me, Cassie," Heath says firmly. "I look at you and I see a beautiful, feisty, ridiculously stubborn, adorable woman who I would love to be my forever."

"I have to go. I'll see you at the rehearsal."

Heath starts to reach out for my hands but stops himself. "But we're good, right, Shortbread?"

"Yeah, Snakebait." Tears fill my eyes and all I want to do is run. "We're good."

"Cass, you're about to cry. Cry on me."

"No." I wipe my eyes with my sleeve and turn around. "I have to go."

I'm halfway to running when I reach the aquarium's exit, and I'm not certain, but I think I hear Heath call out after me.

I look over my shoulder, expecting him to be behind me.

No one.

My phone beeps, alerting me to a text. I look at it.

HEATH: I'M NOT GOING ANYWHERE, SHORTBREAD.

PROMISE. I'll SEE YOU AT THE REHEARSAL. <3

For some stupid reason, seeing Heath use an old school emoticon heart instead of a newfangled emoji sends me into a fit of laughter. I laugh and cry in my car, so confused as to why I can't ignore all the fears and doubts and just admit to being his girlfriend.

Two months, I think. How hard can it be to keep my distance from Heath until March?

If this designated period of contemplation works like I hope it will, I'll accept and know with every fiber of my being that Heath and I belong together.

Thirty-One

Heath

"We scared her away, Dad."

"No, she just needs time to think."

Home from the aquarium, Diesel and I toss a foam football back and forth in the living room. We figured that we needed something mundane yet low-key relaxing to do before bed.

"But girls can take forever to think," Diesel says. "That's what you told me one time. Cassie might never be done thinking."

"Maybe. But she hesitated to walk away. I think she almost cried."

"She did?"

"Almost."

Diesel pauses with the ball in hand, tossing it to himself a few times before throwing it back to me. "Maybe she likes living in a house alone with her dog and no one else."

"Yeah." I give him a tired smile. "Maybe."

Our game continues in silence for a bit, Diesel aiming the

ball toward my face more often than I like.

"Dad?"

"Yeah?"

"Was I invited to Miss Layton's wedding?"

"You were. But you don't have to go. I know that's probably not what any kid wants to sit through."

"Then I don't want to."

"Is it because you hate dressing up or what?"

"No. If you and Cassie see each other again and you end up kissing her, it'll be more romantic if I'm not there."

I laugh. "Thanks, Dees. But she still might not be ready for a kiss."

"But what if she is? What if she finishes her thinking and wants to be your serious girlfriend?"

"Then I guess Cassie and I will have the special moment I've wanted since first meeting her in ninth grade."

"And if she chokes on a cookie, Dad, do the Heimlich. Don't forget that."

"I will," I say, rolling my eyes at him. "Appreciate the reminder, dude."

"You're welcome."

Another five minutes of throwing the ball goes by before Diesel decides to hold onto it and dash away to his room. I sigh, thinking of Cassie and wondering how she's feeling right now. I check my phone and don't see any texts from her.

"Dad!" Diesel yells from his room.

"What?" I say back.

"You should wear something extra cool to the wedding rehearsal. Something to make Cassie excited to see you."

I collapse onto the couch, staring up at the ceiling. "Yeah, Dees? Like what?"

"Maybe more leather. Or something else like you wore when you were in high school."

I laugh as I listen to Diesel start listing "cool" things I could wear, thinking he's just entertaining himself at this point. I glance at a small mirror hung next to the bookshelf, forgetting that I even had put one there, and a fantastic idea blasts into my head.

"Hey, Diesel," I say, getting up and approaching the mirror, "what do you think Cassie would say if I got my ears pierced again?"

"I don't know."

"I think I should. Give her a little throwback to shake her up at the rehearsal dinner."

"Daaaad," Diesel says, drawing out my name in a whine. He comes up behind me as I turn around to look at him.

"What?" I ask. "What's bad about that?"

"No more pranks, Dad! She'll hate you."

"It's not a prank, Dees." I smooth the sides of my hair, smiling as I recall the mornings when I spent an extra ten minutes before school double-checking the combo of my slick hair and badass earrings.

"Are you sure you're not gonna do a prank?" Diesel asks. "You're smiling like I do when I make up a scheme."

"Not a prank," I say, bending to look straight in his eyes. "But I tell you what, Diesel, I will do anything and everything to make Cassie smile."

Diesel smiles back. "Then do it, Dad."

I look back at my reflection.

You got this, Deitrich. Take the wedding rehearsal by storm.

Cassie

I've spent the past several weeks baking like crazy, finishing my photo albums, and running three days a week. And now it's the night before the wedding rehearsal.

I see Heath tomorrow.

"I'm going crazy," I say to myself. "If I can just let Heath kiss me, maybe I'll feel definite about us being together."

Sleepless In Seattle is playing in the background—the third time I've watched it today. My half-eaten bowl of Cocoa Puffs is on the coffee table. I'm exhausted but can't sleep.

Odessa jumps off the couch, perking her ears and looking at me with "I totally hear you" eyes.

"Diesel really likes you," I say to her. "He'd love if I kept bringing you over to their house."

I look up at the ceiling, struggling to determine for the ten millionth time if the pros truly outweigh the cons of allowing love to win.

"I honestly do like being around Diesel too." I roll over, seeing if Odessa is still listening to me. "He's a cute kid and I love watching Heath be such an amazing dad to him."

A serious relationship again after years of being single? Ugh. I don't know.

Sixteen-year-old Cassie would be sorely disappointed in me and my hardcore attraction.

But when I close my eyes and breathe in the swirling mix of what was our youth—classic embarrassment, bitter rivalries, forgetting locker combinations, PE, admittedly hilarious pranks during assemblies—I can only conclude that it was because of Heath's constant troublemaking that gave me the inspiration for the wild, epic adventures I later experienced in my adult life.

I really owe him a kiss for that. I mean, I'm not saying I monstrously crave one... but yeah, maybe I do.

While looking through the pictures of us on my phone—all the silly ones that Heath insisted that we take together—my face grows hot and my heart pounds in my head.

If I'm not careful, I think, I will be the one to humiliate myself at the rehearsal dinner instead of Heath humiliating me. And I know he would find that hilarious and cute.

Thirty-Three

Heath

I have no idea why the rehearsal is taking place inside of a school auditorium instead of at the actual chosen venue several miles away. The thought of it bothers my brain until I see Cassie walk in with Ariana. The entire wedding party was forced to wear matching yellow and silver shirts with some awfully-designed made-up logo on the front—Cass looks so adorable in hers though.

"Heath," Ian says, motioning for myself and the other two groomsmen to move in close, "do you think it's gonna rain tomorrow?"

"What do you mean?"

"Well, me, Todd, and Zak know how you still like to predict weather. You always said it would rain back in the day and half the time you were right. Let's see what happens tomorrow."

"And what? Are we betting on this?"

"We all say you give us sixty bucks if it doesn't rain."

I look at the confidence in Todd and Zak's eyes and the slight sourness on Ian's face. "Ariana chewed you out about something, huh?"

"Just do the bet, Heath."

"Alright." We high-five each other, and then I grin when Cassie approaches me.

I'm hoping I can easily pick up from where we left off two months ago at the aquarium—but in a more fun-spirited way. "Hey, Cass," I say, "I gotta show you something."

Cassie quickly looks back at Ariana, seeming concerned that she'll get yelled at, but joins me in the middle of the makeshift aisle. "Yeah? What've you got?"

"Look closely," I say. I do a little spin and make a sweeping motion to my head and face. "Notice anything different?"

"Oh my…" She swallows hard, looking like she's just seen a ten-eyed green ghost. "You didn't."

"I did!" I say. "The earrings! It's epic, right!?"

Cassie grabs my arm, her voice coming out in a squeaky whisper—I think she's just as excited and hyper as I am. "Heath, when did you do this?"

"Three weeks ago. I got the silver hoop earrings because they remind me of the style I used to wear." I flick one of her dangly stacked hoop earrings and say, "They kind of match yours, don't you think?"

"You just had to become overtly romantic, didn't you?"

"Well, I missed wearing them."

"You wore earrings for two years as a teenager. Why'd you have to get into it again?" Cassie looks like she's about to growl at me but instead bites her lip and aggressively runs her fingers through her hair. "Nothing in society says you have to have pierced ears to be cool."

"I know," I say proudly, "And I know you love it."

"Heath, I do not need this kind of distraction right now. I don't want to be feeling all giggly and blushing and teenagery with you showing off like the darn stud you are!"

"Cassie! Come here."

We look at Ariana who's standing on a chair in order to get people's attention. She points at Cassie and says, "We have to go over something right now. All of us girls."

Cassie blows out a sigh, smiles at me, then starts heading back toward Ariana. But I'm not ready for her to have her little meeting with the other bridesmaids—whatever Ariana has to say is going to be dull and not as entertaining as my earrings.

"Psst, Cass! Cass!"

"What?" she snaps, looking over her shoulder at me.

I grin and crook a finger for her to come in close. "I know you have a list of mature things to discuss with the other ladies, but I have to tell you one more important thing."

Casssie rolls her eyes and gestures to Ariana that she'll be there in another minute. She lets me lead her to a private corner. "What is it, Heath? You do know we are all adults in our forties at a wedding rehearsal, right? Why are you making me feel like I'm being called to the principal's office?"

"I want us to make a bet, Shortbread."

"A bet about what?"

"Rain."

"Rain?"

"I think there will be a downpour right after the ceremony tomorrow but Ian and the other guys think it won't rain. I need you to join in on this."

"There's no way it's going to rain, Heath. Have you seen the weather report for the next ten days?"

"It's totally wrong. It's going to rain and I need you to pick a side. I wanna make this interesting with you."

"Interesting, sure," she scoffs, tilting her head at me. "I predict that it will not rain a single drop."

"And I say it will be a massive downpour."

Cassie's annoyed expression morphs into a sly smile. "All right, Snakebait, I know EXACTLY how to make this a perfectly outlandish and interesting bet."

"Do tell."

"If I win," she says, "we will have nothing but breakfast dates for three more months, and there is still no sitting together on the same piece of furniture."

"And if I win, Shortbread, we get to go on dates at any time of the day, you sit and cuddle on the couch with me without a complaint, AND we kiss."

"Reasonable terms," Cassie says with a nonchalant air. She turns to go where Ariana is frantically motioning for her, but gives me a lingering look over her shoulder and winks.

Wow, I think, she is in a playful mood today. This bet we just made doesn't make any sense at all yet she just went along with it. I'm sort of speechless. And crazy in love.

Thirty-Four

Cassie

Once we've all sat down at a long table in the sushi restaurant—quite an unusual place for a rehearsal dinner—I force myself to not think about how badly I want to be in Heath's arms.

He just HAD to throw the pirate earrings back in and lure me into a stupid but rather ingenious bet when he knows I'm trying to maintain a tiny bit of grown woman sanity.

"Cassie, I'm really glad you and Heath have ended the feud. Nice to see you two as friends."

I smile at Ariana, ready to vocalize my agreement, but I'm stopped by an incredibly harsh kick from under the table. Ariana sees my expression change to a scowl and we both look across the way at Heath who's wearing a huge grin.

"You did not just do that," I say.

"I sure did, Shortbread."

"Seriously, guys." Ariana rolls her eyes and stands up with her glass of wine. "I am not sitting here and getting in the middle of whatever is about to go down."

"Go ahead and leave," Heath tells her, "but you'll miss out on some great entertainment."

"Don't want it," Ariana calls back.

Within a few minutes, one of Ariana's family members starts giving some highly eloquent speech—I don't know who they are or pay any attention to it because of how Heath is making kissy faces at me. And I happen to notice that everyone in the wedding party has moved away from Heath and I—I guess we look like trouble to them. But at least now we can have a conversation by ourselves in a corner and not be even more embarrassing.

"You're not gonna win," I say.

"But how would you like to be kissed when I do?"

"Just shush, Heath. Everyone here is gonna be pissed that we're stealing their thunder."

Heath gives an extremely sly look to the far side of the table and waves at Ariana and Ian who are sitting close together. He gestures for me to look in their direction, and I do, seeing Ariana glowering at us and mouthing "use your inside voices".

I'm not sure it's the fact that I'm being treated like a kid in her class or what, but getting scolded in that way brings out a sudden bright spark of mischief in me, and without explaining it to Heath, I slide down in my chair and kick him in the leg as hard as I can, causing the table to shift.

All he does is laugh. A snort-laugh. "Can't wait to see you tomorrow, Cass. In all your glamorous glory."

"You can't ogle me the whole time. It's Ariana and Ian's big moment, not ours."

"I know. And if it does rain after the ceremony, you better brace yourself for an epic kiss."

"And if it doesn't rain?" I ask him. "What'll you do then? Mope?"

"No. I'll enjoy dancing with you. If all I get to do for the next few months is more breakfast dates and staring into your sweet eyes, Cass, that's just fine with me."

"Me too," I say. "Totally fine with that."

I'm totally lying. I want Heath to kiss me now.

But for old time's sake, I pretend to be his rival.

"I got this competition wrapped up," I say, showing him the weather app on my phone. "Nothing but clear skies."

Heath just smiles and takes a bite of his rice. I do the same.

We try to act mature through the rest of the dinner so as not to further disrupt the classy ambiance, but, of course, we can't help but continue to trade sly looks and kick each other under the table.

Nothing tops the entertainment level of this evening, I think. *Nothing. Heath is my best friend.*

Thirty-Five

Heath

The sky on the morning of Ariana and Ian's wedding is a disappointing bright blue hue. Hardly a breeze. Few clouds. But if I've learned anything about my life, it's that things can change in an instant—like winning a bet in an unlikely circumstance.

I pace in the groomsman dressing room after putting on my suit, checking all angles of myself in the mirror. It's honestly the first time in my entire life I've put on a suit as fancy as this one and I actually like how it looks. I'm glad to just be able to focus on my role of walking a bridesmaid down the aisle.

The feisty, beloved bridesmaid by the name of Cassie Wicker. My soulmate.

"Hey, Ian, mind if I go find Cassie?"

"Nope. On my way to see Ariana." He grins at me. "Doing the whole first look thing."

"Cool," I say. "I'll see you out there."

"Yeah. Just don't miss your cue or Arry will yell at both of us."

I nod at him and jog out the back door of the farmhouse, my head on a swivel.

Wanna see Cassie in her glamorous form. Just me and her.

I take out my phone and text: **Hey, Cass. Feel like meeting up before the ceremony?**

I wait for a response, leaning against the largest gazebo on the property. The setting is a mix of rustic farmland and flowery meadow, and it couldn't be a better place to lay my eyes on a dolled up Cassie.

My phone beeps and I look at the text.

CASSIE: Turn around.

I lose my breath for a second before looking over my shoulder. I fully turn around as she approaches from the opposite side of the gazebo, amused at her grumbling as she walks in high heels.

"Hi, Heath." She does a little spin to show off her dress. "First time you see me in a dress. The color's lousy but it does have pockets. Pockets are always a plus."

I laugh at her excitement over the pockets and take in her smoking figure. "You're beautiful in anything you wear, Cass."

"That's sweet."

"It's just the truth," I say. "What do you think of me in a suit? First time you see me in something like this."

"Yeah." She grins. "You're rocking it, Heath."

"Thanks." I get chills thinking about how Cassie and I are seeing each other at the exact same time as the bride and groom are having their first look moment. "Do the pirate earrings clash with my fancy threads?"

"No," Cassie says with a giggle. She tilts her head, briefly looks at the ground, and looks back at me while adjusting her glasses. "It's hot."

Then I'm doing something right, I think.

I smile, take her arm in mine, and point toward where the music has just started. "Looks like we gotta start heading over there."

"Yeah," she says. "Or we're dead meat."

"Yeah."

I keep looking at Cassie as she stares back. The sassy glee in her gorgeous eyes is killing me. And she knows it.

Thirty-Six

Cassie

I did not expect to be feeling so bashful walking down the aisle with Heath. He is quite a heartthrob and on his best behavior, but I know he could flip the script at any minute.

Snakebait and Shortbread arm in arm. No more desire for revenge. Who would've thought?

"Heath," I say through my exaggerate-for-the-cameras smile, "I thought I'd wanna kill you in this moment."

"And you wanna jump my bones now, huh?"

"No, I am not thinking that."

Heath grins and presses his arm tighter against mine. "I feel like I'm taking you to prom."

"I can imagine how horrible that would've been," I say, embarrassed by how much I feel myself regressing in this moment.

"Yeah. I'd have tried to slap your butt so many times."

"Oh, for goodness sake, Heath," I loudly whisper as we split up to stand in our respective positions at the altar.

I hear him cover a laugh with a cough and I fiddle with my bouquet.

Flip hair. Smile in sync with the other bridesmaids. Do not look at him.

If I look in Heath's direction while we're up here, I just know he will mess up my poker face. I don't want to be the one crazy bridesmaid who's caught on camera snort-laughing because of a stupidly cute, immature man who I am dying to kiss.

Thirty-Seven

Heath

I've never seen Cassie fidget so much. She's probably thinking about the bet in the midst of avoiding direct eye contact with me.

C'mon, Shortbread, just look in my eyes for a minute! Just one minute!

I look up at the sky, grinning at the clouds rolling closer and closer. There is a tinge of gray in them. The breeze feels snappier.

Look at me, Shortbread, c'mon.

I stare past Ian and Ariana as they read their vows, my undivided attention locked in on Cassie and her twitchy smile.

I'm hoping she kisses me back—I can't crave anything more right now than her soft mouth pressed to mine.

I bite my lip at the thought and see Cassie's eyes shift to my direction. Her expression is different than it has been—love, adoration, joy.

She craves me too.

"C'mon, rain," I whisper to the sky. "You got this. We're a team. Downpour just for me."

I know a rainstorm will piss off everyone standing out here in their best suits and dresses, but the payoff is everything and more. I feel like a giddy, unhinged doofus who can't stop his prolonged looks at the clouds and who won't stop shifting from one foot to the other like he's a kindergartner trying to avoid running to the bathroom.

Looking over at Cassie again, I honestly admire her for wearing a dress that she hates and I randomly find myself thinking back to the last moment that I saw Cassie when we were young—our high school graduation. Cassie had been surrounded by her family and friends in the first five seconds of exiting the auditorium doors, and my deepest wish at that time was to ask her for a hug and tell her I wanted to be her man.

And I'm so close now, I think. *So close to making up for the awful display in the cafeteria... I want to hold my girl, kiss her, let her know that we are, in fact, meant for each other.*

The recessional music starts up and I get ready to walk with Cassie back up the aisle, thinking I still have a shot at winning the bet as long as the rain comes during the post-ceremony pictures.

"Well, well," Cassie says to me in a flippant tone as I take her arm in mine. "What do you have to say now, Heath? No rain. No thunder or lightning."

"Not yet, Shortbread," I say, "Give it another—"

Then I feel a raindrop.

And another raindrop.

And suddenly.

The rain comes down in sheets.

"Oh. My. Gosh." Cassie's jaw drops as she grabs my arms and stops us in the middle of the grass.

I grin up at the sky, erupting into laughter as everyone around us shrieks and yells out remarks about how the weather wasn't supposed to be bad. The guests and wedding party—minus me and Cassie—run for cover in the reception-designated barn.

"C'mon, Cass!"

Thunder rumbles as Cassie wordlessly accepts my hand and we run to the gazebo. I can hear her giggling.

"Wait, Heath," she says, abruptly pulling away from me. "Wait."

"What?" I ask. I turn, wondering why she doesn't want to get under the eave of the gazebo. "Aren't you cold?"

"I have to tell you something."

"Yeah?"

"Yeah. But I need you to come here."

"Okay," I say, moving back out into the storm. "What is it, Cass?"

Thirty-Eight

Cassie

Head to toe soaked in this pelting rain—the weather report showed nothing of the kind. My dress is stuck to my body like Gorilla Glue and my nifty hairstyle is totally wilted and stringy.

Wonderful, romantic, ridiculous, beautiful. I'm happy. So, so, happy.

I smile up at the rain and look back at Heath. "I lost the bet."

"Oh, I don't know," Heath teases. "Judging by the look in your eyes I think you just won."

I can't believe I feel love for this man. Overwhelming love. Overwhelming desire to be in his life.

"Kiss me, Snakebait," I say.

He grins, looking absolutely radiant in the pouring rain. "If you insist, Shortbread."

"I do."

Heath tilts his head, looking from my eyes to my mouth, and reaches to touch my hair. He slowly entangles his fingers in it, pulling my face to his, breathing softly on my lips. And he kisses me. The most gentle, comforting, and tingle-inducing kiss I've had in my life.

"You're made for me, Shortbread," he whispers before we kiss again. "I can't live without you."

"Undoubtedly," I whisper back. "You've got me forever, Snakebait."

We look at each other as we sway in the rain, Heath spontaneously dipping me and pulling me back to him in the tightest embrace.

"What do you think?" he asks. "Should we ditch the reception and run off into the wild blue?"

"No. I wanna dance with you right here."

"You got it, baby." He brushes damp hair from my eyes and smiles.

I smile back, slowly moving with him into the protection of the gazebo. I pull my phone out from my dress pocket, put one of the earbuds in my ear, and give Heath the other one. He looks confused but continues to gaze lovingly at me as I scroll through and land on a song.

"Kids" by OneRepublic.

Heath's grin widens as he sings along for a few seconds. He playfully spins me around before drawing me in for a long, deep kiss that is very reminiscent of the sloppy one he gave me in the cafeteria—but in the best way possible.

Snakebait loves Shortbread. If there's a truer statement to be said, I don't know what it is.

The pinnacle of adventure. Dancing in the middle of a storm with the guy that I never thought I'd want to be mine.

Heath Alun Deitrich. My life. My love. My favorite person in the world.

About the Author

Han M Greenbarg has been in love with writing fiction since childhood. She is an avid coffee drinker, proud dog mom, and lover of a variety of music and movies. She achieves her biggest jolts of inspiration while being out in nature, and especially enjoys crafting parallel fantasy worlds, snappy dialogue, and sweet, dry-humored characters.

You can connect with me on:

- https://www.instagram.com/hanmgreenbargauthor

Elf Bat Book One Kiah

Twelve years after the ruthless massacre of his parents and most of his kin, eighteen-year-old Elf Bat Kiah lives a life of internalized grief and solitude in his family's cave. The arrival of Fly, a reckless purebred Elf maiden, sparks the flame for revenge and a resurgence of the Bats.

Elf Bat Book Two Sacrifice

The revenge of the Elf Bats has begun in Sidhovvn, each Bat warrior facing down the count who carried out the ruthless slaughter of their family. But in the midst of seeking justice against the purebred king and his soldiers, the sudden emergence of Fly's demon-driven adoptive mother Ixetmori proves to be the bigger test of wills, and the defining moment of what it means to be courageous.

Chehnuh

Year 2018. Chehnuh, a half-elven and sole survivor of his people's genocide, resides quietly in a remote cabin in the Sierra Nevada mountains. No one knows how he came to the United States. No one knows that he is part Elf. He is a mystery to all who meet him until a young widowed mother interrupts his peaceful life with a baby and the shadow of a deadly stalker, forever changing how Chehnuh sees his own past, humanity, and the heroic role he has yet to play in today's world.

Byrne

Imagination is survival. That's what he tells them. Full of weird quirks and crazy story ideas, novelist Maddox Byrne can't figure out how to connect with normal people. Ever since the lockdown began and the residents of Tower 881 were trapped together, all he's wanted was to keep morale high and finally get the woman of his dreams to notice him. But every person has a breaking point. Every person longs for what they can't have. How long can humanity live in distrust and paranoia? How long before every person loses their mind? Imagination. Imagination is survival. But can it really save us?

Firemartenn

Blamed for his father's death and the doom of Ateinekus, fifteen-year-old Jet must prove his worth as Firemartenn to the village elders. But the fire dragon king won't let just anyone reach the sacred Ackellhnn's sapphire. Jet has to play by Feuskarg's rules in order to save his family and be the hero he's always wanted to be.

Riverduna

Year 2098. Seventeen-year-old Riverduna lives carefree in Nameus, enjoying the peace of the rooftops and her attic books. But loneliness and a desire for adventure draws her toward the Paedors. When she is given the chance to visit Dredgar, her view of both worlds is turned upside down. Can she learn the ways of the streets without losing her Sky heart to darkness?

Champion pit fighter Dunn knows every survival trick on the streets, but he fears for the future of his baby sister and all the children in the city. Violence between district gangs is escalating each day with no end in sight. Can he find a way to change the lawlessness and brutality of Dredgar before more of his loved ones are killed?

When their paths cross, Riverduna and Dunn realize that it's up to them to take on the harrowing journey to discover the truth about their worlds… and to find peace and love in the darkest of places.

Scurts Flightplan

Revenge is best served warm, so says my associate Robbie Decker. Kill your demons. They won't plague you again. Really. Then how do you explain my current situation? Locked up in the company of airport eccentrics, friend to a pardoned killer, and pacing the million degree terminal with my wine-drunk therapist. Three months left to live…and I think I got blood on my hands. Talk about your midlife crisis. Where did I go wrong?—From The Journal of Damon Scurto

Vow Of The Silent Kindred

We aren't just best friends. We're kindred spirits. Never felt accepted by anyone on this crazy planet called Earth. Dressed up as our own imaginative characters Arrowswan and Jaeger Bowen, we take on the adventure of life and make it ours. No matter what the haters say. Our friends may toss in some wild schemes, and our families may have their own dreams for us, but we never give up on each other. The love story you didn't know you needed. A sweet and quirky romantic comedy full of memorable characters, relatable mishaps, and all the highs and lows of this unpredictable life. It may not be easy, but it is worth the fight.

Dankaehn: Book One Of The Dankaehn Trilogy

Seventeen-year-old Elf Prince Teague has felt like a burden on his family and kingdom since birth. After the sudden death of his granda, Teague joins his beloved granna to seek a new life outside the royal city. Meeting legendary animal whisperer Titus proves to be the biggest adventure of his life, teaching him all there is to know about the magical traditions of their people's past, and showing Teague just how special he is in the face of adversity.

A coming of age story reminding us all that we each have a purpose in the world, and that no matter how we see ourselves in the present moment, we have the potential to do great things.